BOUND BY A COMMON ENEMY

Tied to the violent Edmund by a betrothal contract, Elizabeth Farrell gains an unexpected opportunity for deliverance when their bridal party is stopped in the forest by a band of men. William Downes offers to pay off her contract — if she will enter a temporary marriage of convenience with him instead. Scarred by his past, William refuses to consider marrying for love, but needs a bride to protect both his sister's illegitimate child and the family's land. Will Elizabeth accept the bargain?

Books by Lucy Oliver
in the Linford Romance Library:

THE ORCHID

LUCY OLIVER

BOUND BY A COMMON ENEMY

Complete and Unabridged

LINFORD
Leicester

First published in Great Britain in 2015

First Linford Edition
published 2016

*A catalogue record for this book is available
from the British Library.*

ISBN 978–1–4448–2909–9

Published by
F. A. Thorpe (Publishing)
Anstey, Leicestershire

Set by Words & Graphics Ltd.
Anstey, Leicestershire
Printed and bound in Great Britain by
T. J. International Ltd., Padstow, Cornwall

This book is printed on acid-free paper

1

Forest of Dean, England. 1448

'Halt!'

The shout came from the undergrowth lining the forest path. Elizabeth Farrell yanked her reins as the animal tossed its head and sidestepped, her crimson riding gown tangling in her stirrups. Was it outlaws? The last innkeeper had tried to warn her that the forest was dangerous, though she hadn't cared enough at the time to listen.

The bushes rustled ahead and a man stepped out, wearing a dark doublet and gripping a long sword, the tip glinting under the weak autumn sun. Elizabeth squeezed her legs, but a twig cracked behind her; looking over her shoulder, her mouth fell open. Five men stood grimly behind her, cudgels clutched in their hands.

'Run!' she shouted to her servants, who trailed behind her on their mules. However, they stayed motionless, as if they had grown roots in the manner of the trees around them. Elizabeth glanced at her husband-to-be, and her lip curled. Edmund sat frozen on his mount, his eyes wide and blinking like a baby mouse's.

He had a sword, so why didn't he act? They were surrounded. As much as she didn't want to marry Edmund, having her throat slit by outlaws wouldn't be a better option. She looked at the man in front of her.

'What do you want?' she said.

He stepped closer and she stilled her horse. Now wasn't the time for panic; he had a grim look in his eyes.

'Do you want gold?'

His heavy boots snapped the twigs on the forest floor as he stepped forward to stare at her — his dark brown eyes menacing and chin rough with stubble. The man pushed back the sleeves of his doublet, showing arms hard with muscle. What was he going to do?

'Who are you?' she said.

'He's nobody, just a common thief,' Edmund said.

'Your companion knows me, mistress.'

'I last saw you, Will Downes, crawling down the steps of my house,' Edmund said. 'Why are you stopping my wife and me? Was one beating not enough?'

Elizabeth opened her mouth to protest that they were not yet wed, then raised a hand to touch a painful bruise on her cheek. Will Downes narrowed his eyes with a fleeting expression of recognition, followed by a tightening of his mouth.

'Who are you, my lady?'

'She is none of your concern,' Edmund said.

Will pointed to a strongbox tied to the pack mules. 'Take that chest, Robert.'

A well-built man with reddish hair stepped forward, his dagger raised.

Elizabeth stared at the box and her stomach clenched.

'Please not that; it's all the money I have.'

The man shrugged and sawed through the leather straps attaching it to the mule, then pulled the box to the forest floor with a thud that echoed through the trees. Elizabeth's hands whitened on her reins. How dare they steal from her!

'Edmund!' she said. 'Are you going to let these men rob us? Give me your sword, if you won't use it.'

The man laughed. 'Shamed by a woman, Edmund. I don't envy you her in your marriage bed.'

Edmund's teeth drew back from his lips, and Elizabeth shuddered. She had many times seen that look. Why had she been so foolish as to agree to marry the man? Inhaling deeply, she remembered holding her cousin's tiny baby in her arms, breathing in the soft, warm, milky scent. Her desire to be a mother had driven her to become betrothed to a man she barely knew.

Edmund drew his sword and, with a cry, lashed out at Will Downes, who caught the blow with his own blade. The loud clash sent birds flying from the trees around them and Elizabeth gripped her reins tight. She needed to escape, and with luck, the two men would destroy each other.

Edmund jerked as a powerful strike almost unseated him. Will's eyes darkened and he jumped forward, his weapon held high. Edmund yanked his reins and tried to turn the horse, but he was too late and Will brought his weapon down in a hard stab against Edmund's thigh. Blood spurted over his breeches, dripping onto the forest floor in a claret rain, before Will slashed the sword up and sliced Edmund's hand.

Elizabeth twisted away, nausea rising in her throat. She glanced at the other men, but they were watching the fight, their cudgels at the ready. Edmund wouldn't stand much of a chance if he managed to kill this Will Downes. No one was looking at her, though;

tightening her legs, she trotted her horse into the forest.

'Hey!' It was the man with reddish hair. 'Stay with your servants. Don't go in there alone.'

She snorted. Did he think she was an idiot? How safe would she be back in the glen? And the servants would not help her — they were Edmund's and bound to his bidding. There must be a town somewhere, or other travellers she could follow. If it fell silent behind her, she could always creep back and check the packs for coins missed by the robbers.

However, a few yards into the trees, the sound of galloping hooves echoed through the forest and she looked back. It was Edmund on his battle-trained destrier, charging straight towards her. Behind him, on foot, ran the brown-eyed man.

'Edmund, you're going to hit me!' she said, pulling hard on her horse's mouth, but her trembling mare refused to move. There wasn't time to dismount and, hunching her shoulders, she braced herself. The powerful warhorse crashed into her mount's haunches and her horse reared, throwing her face against its neck, crushing her mouth. She screamed as bright red blood dripped onto the animal's hide, and as her hands slipped on the reins, she fell sideways under its iron-shod hooves.

A hand gripped her shoulder and dragged her out.

'Hurt?' a man's voice said.

It was William Downes. Elizabeth stared up at him from her knees, warm blood creeping down her face, hard twigs thrust into her leg. The pounding hooves could have split his skull. She tried to thank him, but groaned as her lip throbbed.

'Your companion has vanished into the forest,' he said. 'You'd best go after him.'

His hands touched her skirts as he tried to help her up, but it reminded her of Edmund's hard fingers.

'Let me go!' she said, and thrust her

7

elbow into his stomach. He grabbed her shoulder and pulled her towards her horse.

'Get up, mistress! Else you'll be stranded here.'

He reached for her horse's reins, but the animal snorted and lashed out with its hooves, forcing him to jump backwards.

'What type of untamed monster are you riding?' he said.

Wiping blood from her face, Elizabeth stared open-mouthed at the glen a few yards away.

'Where are the servants and mule train?'

'They fled after Edmund, while you were falling from your horse. You must go after and catch them up.'

She looked into the trees at the dark, shadowed undergrowth and deep bracken.

'She'll never find them, my lord,' the reddish-haired man said.

William cursed. 'We're stuck with her then, Robert.'

'What shall we do with her?'

'She can't be left here alone. Doesn't look the type to survive on river-water and rabbits.'

Elizabeth gasped. 'I won't tell! Please let me go, I've done you no harm.'

They were going to take her from the path and kill her under the green trees like a hunted stag. She grabbed the hem of her dress and bolted into the forest.

Broken twigs snapped under her shoes and brambles scratched her arms, ripping into the skin. She ignored them, pushing through the trees, craning her head for a glimpse of movement. Where could she hide? She had to avoid Edmund, too, since he would be as likely to kill her as these outlaws. A rustle of leaves came from ahead. Was it the servants? She quickened her pace.

Then bushes jerked violently to the side and a squeal, loud and human-like, echoed through the trees. She froze, hand raised to her mouth. The bracken trembled a few feet away and she

9

stepped back, sweating, mouth dry. What terror lay ahead?

'Stay still,' a voice said behind her.

The dark-haired man stood in the bushes watching her, sword drawn. 'I'm not going to hurt you.'

She panted, backing away from him. Did he take her for a fool?

'Come here please, my lady.' His voice was controlled. 'That was a wild boar.'

'I'd rather a bristled pig to you. And there aren't boar in the forests anymore.'

He smiled. 'Tell him that.'

A huge black pig burst out from the undergrowth beside her, thrashing its white tusks and grunting. Elizabeth cried out and jumped back. It was bigger than she had expected. Her nostrils filled with a foul, musky reek. Will leapt over a fallen tree and threw himself in front of her, stabbing down with his sword. The animal screamed and backed away, mouth open, drool dripping from its jaws.

'Go!' he said. 'Before I turn you into stew.'

It bolted into the undergrowth. Wiping sweat from her face, she looked at him. There was no point in running; he could outpace her. Her head whirled and she grasped the tree behind for her support; she'd had no food today. Edmund hadn't allowed her.

'Are you all right?' the man said. 'Mistress?'

She slumped against the trunk, black spots in front of her eyes and nausea rising from her stomach.

★   ★   ★

Fur brushed her face, strong arms held her. Was it her uncle? Dazed, Elizabeth raised her head. It was the outlaw! What was he going to do? Would anyone hear her if she screamed? Struggling, she thrust her elbow back again, and was rewarded by a cry. Then the man's arms withdraw, dropping her to the floor. She landed with a thud and scowling, glared up from the fallen leaves, her face level with his leather riding boots.

He stepped back. 'You're lucky I came after you, mistress. Now get up and stay close, for your own safety.' He drew his sword.

'My safety? You're an outlaw!' she said.

'Outlaw? No, I'm Lord William Downes, Baron of Shorecross. I don't know who you are, but I mean you no ill-will. Come, we'll return to the others.'

'Am I a hostage?'

'No, but you are under my protection.'

Elizabeth straightened her skirt, aware of the blood smeared over her lip and the brambles in her hair. Around her, the trees darkened under the setting sun and the air filled with the sharpness of a coming frost. She had no weapons, food, or means to make a fire.

'You'll be lost before you get ten paces,' he said. 'We'll reach the castle of

St Briavels tomorrow; you can get help there.'

She had no choice but to trust him. 'Please escort me back to my horse.'

'Of course, and if you do try to run again, I'd take your gown off first.'

Elizabeth looked down at her riding habit. It was bright red. No wonder she hadn't got far.

★ ★ ★

In the clearing, Robert stood stroking her horse.

'Got her, my lord,' he said. 'Wonderful animal, great legs; rather skittish, though.'

'Like its owner,' Will said.

'What?' Elizabeth said.

He grinned.

'We need to get moving, my lord, night draws close,' Robert said. 'We fetched our mounts and pack mules while you were running after the girl.' He glanced at her with exasperation.

Elizabeth glared back. What had he

expected her to do? Will reached for the bridle of a dark bay animal tied to a tree.

'We'll lead the horses, the path narrows here.'

Elizabeth looked at the track thick with mud and puddles. She wore riding shoes and a long habit, and her muscles ached. If the outlaws were going to drag her down there, she wasn't going to make it easy for them.

'You lead my horse,' she said. 'Since you're the reason I fell off it.'

He hesitated and looked at her face, which she knew was bruised and blood-stained. Handing his own mount to a servant, he took her reins and offered his other arm. Her cheeks burned and she shook her head.

'Take it,' he said. 'Else we'll never get out of here. And I think we can dispense with formalities; my friends call me Will.' He raised his eyebrows.

'My name is my own concern.'

Her legs hurt and there was a sharp pain in her knee. It dented her pride to rely on him, but she'd have to take his arm. Elizabeth took it, and glanced down at the costly silver thread embroidering the black sleeve. Maybe he spoke the truth about who he was — but why would a lord rob travellers? If he was caught, he would be hanged.

'Where were you going, mystery lady?' he said. 'What kin do you have? I'm afraid I won't take you back to your husband; I couldn't be that cruel to anyone.'

'I'm not friendless; my absence will be noticed. And he's not my husband. I was due to marry him tomorrow.'

'I suspect I've ruined your wedding day.'

Elizabeth thought about Edmund's last words, spat at her in fury.

We are contractually betrothed, he had said. *And if you leave, I'll make your uncle pay the contract fee.*

She tightened her lips. Edmund hadn't even waited until they were married to show his true colours; he knew she was trapped, since her uncle had no means to pay.

Elizabeth glanced at Will as he strode beside her, leather reins wrapped around his hand as her horse walked peacefully behind. Mud clung to her shoes, softening her step, and a bird trilled in the trees. She breathed in the fresh woodland scent of wet vegetation and decomposing leaves.

'How do you know Edmund?' she said.

Will drew his sword and slashed down at the brambles. 'We are relatives — distant ones, thankfully. What are you doing marrying him? Do you know his character?'

Her hand went to the bruise on her cheek. 'It has nothing to do with you.' She remembered the baby she had pictured in its cradle. Rather than her own home and family, would she now remain a permanent and unwelcome guest at her aunt's house? To be forever grateful and meek?

Will glanced at her. 'Did you know your betrothed is already married?'

She stopped. 'What?'

'Edmund wed my sister Joan in a private ceremony, which he now denies.'

She stood still. 'Married? He is a bigamist? I was marrying a bigamist?'

'The wedding can't be proved, so I imagine he considers himself free to wed again. Meanwhile, Joan is now pregnant and deserted.' He glanced at her. 'My sister wouldn't have lain with him if she hadn't believed herself married.'

'That's terrible.' Elizabeth raised a hand to her mouth. No wonder Will hated Edmund. Joan's life was ruined; no man would wed her now. 'Will Edmund give the baby his name?'

'He must never find out about the child.' He looked at her sharply. 'I'm trusting you not to tell him.'

'I loathe him as much as you do.' She shivered, wistful for the comfort of her uncle's arm across her shoulder. The world beyond his farm was proving to be an unpleasant place.

'Take my mantle.' Will unfastened the

17

clasp and draped it over her shoulders. 'Were you forced into the marriage?'

She stayed silent.

'It's in your interests to talk to me. We have a common enemy. I can't believe you loved him, not a man such as he.'

'I was a fool. I didn't love him, but I believed he cared for me. While we were courting, he treated me well, and I needed to marry. The town monastery took half my uncle's farmland, and my upkeep had become a burden.'

Will frowned. 'Why would Edmund marry you if you had no money?'

She pressed her lips together.

'I don't know. My mother left me a farm in the West Country, but it's poor soil and worth little. The locals use the fields for grazing their animals on.' She lifted her chin as she remembered her land. 'I am going to travel there now and take possession of it, for I won't return to Edmund.'

'You're going to farm it by yourself?' His lips quirked upwards.

'It is common for wives to take care of their husband's estates while they are away at war.'

'Yes, but they are married and have more freedom.'

'Wives have no freedom: Edmund showed me that. Once we wed, he can do anything he wants. I have more freedom as a spinster.'

'To do what? If you were a working woman, you could take a trade, but as a highborn lady, there is nothing you can do except wed or enter a convent.'

'And I'm doing neither.' She shuddered.

'Then you will starve.'

'Which at least will be my choice! I would have starved under the care of a husband just as effectively as I might do alone.'

Will paused. 'You haven't eaten today?'

'No, nor last night.'

'We had better stop and make some pottage before you faint again.'

'Not until we are further away from

Edmund. I don't want to be caught.'

He grinned. 'So you would rather stay with me?'

She turned her head away. 'I would prefer neither of you, but since I have little choice, I will stay with you until we reach the castle tomorrow.'

'How gracious of you, my lady. We are honoured.'

She moistened her lips, opening her mouth to apologise, but he stalked ahead. She wasn't normally this rude; but, after Edmund, she didn't want any man paying attention to her. Better that Will ignored her, leaving her to stumble along behind. At least she was away from Edmund now, although he would certainly search for her. Whatever his reasons for marrying her, they had been strong enough for him to make the necessary arrangements and escort her to his home. She thought of her new clothes and wedding gown, vanished into the forest with the servants. Likely her maidservant would find a use for them, since the girl had stolen enough trinkets from her already.

Will waited further up the path.

'Careful, there are brambles here,' he said, holding the stinging green plants back with his sword.

'Thank you, and I apologise for speaking out of turn,' she said.

'You're scared, so I hold no grudge. I can imagine what this last week must have been like.'

She looked at him. 'I could have coped with being hit and insulted, if he hadn't chosen to do it in front of the servants, who watched, laughing. He humiliated me and made me look a fool.'

Will sheathed his sword with a rustle. 'Where are your parents?'

'They died of the pestilence when I was twelve, both gone within two days.'

'I'm sorry. It's too common an illness.'

She nodded and looked at her horse. 'I can lead her now.'

'That's all right, my lady. I'm managing fine.' He looked up at the evening sky, glowing between the branches. 'We'll need to stop soon anyway for supper.'

Her stomach rumbled. 'How far is the nearest tavern?'

'There aren't any in the forest; we'll have to camp for the night. You can share our food.'

She stared at him. 'Sleep in the open, surrounded by men?'

'My men won't touch you, and I can guarantee, neither will I.'

'I have never slept outside before.'

'I doubt you have, my lady, but there's no other choice tonight. We can't continue to ride, my servants are exhausted. Don't worry, my men can be trusted; they've been with me for years.'

At least he understood her concerns.

'My lord?' Robert called, pointing into the forest. 'This looks a good place to stop.'

Elizabeth glanced at a large clearing with a charred circle in the centre surrounded by rocks, beside a fallen log covered in bright green mosses. Since she had no choice, she'd have to accept it; and to be honest, it looked cleaner than some of the inns Edmund had made her stay in. She'd feel better if there was another woman in the party, but there wasn't even a serving girl.

'Sit on the log while we set up the camp,' Will said.

Elizabeth slumped down on the trunk. The rotting wood would mark her gown, but she didn't care. Shivering, she pulled the borrowed fur mantle closer around her shoulders and drew a deep breath. This wasn't how she'd expected to spend the day before her wedding. Penniless, deserted and surrounded by outlaws.

'Water?' Will said, coming over towards her, a leather drinking flask in his hand. Unscrewing it, he held it out.

'Thank you.' She wiped the edge, then drank deeply.

'Keep it, we have others,' he said, turning away.

She took out her handkerchief and moistened it, before wiping the blood from her face. Stuffing the hanky away, she watched the servants dicing vegetables, and her stomach rumbled. An owl hooted in the trees above, and the grass rustled by her foot; looking down, she saw a mouse bolt over the small chest the outlaws had dumped on the ground. She stared at the box. Would they give it back to her?

'I've brought you some rugs,' Will said, folding the blankets and laying them on the grass in front of her. His black doublet and hose left him virtually invisible in the shadows. 'Lie down and rest.'

Sitting down, Elizabeth pulled the bottom rug over her legs. The blankets were the softness of a lord's bedding — did she sleep in his covers?

'Comfortable?' he said.

'Yes, but I hope I haven't taken your bed.'

He shook his head, then looked around as a wolf howled, reaching for his sword.

'I think it's further away, my lord,' Robert said. He lifted the pot off the stove and ladled pottage onto thick slices of bread. Will picked up a slice and brought it over to her.

'Eat carefully, it's hot.'

She looked up into his eyes, dark under the shadows, and a sudden heat surged across her body as if she'd moved to close to the fire. His lips parted and his hand trembled slightly, pouring boiling stew over his fingers. He drew in a sharp breath.

'You're burned!' she said, reaching to grab the bread trencher.

He yanked it away from her. 'Robert! The woman needs a plate, she can't eat as we do.'

Robert held out a metal dish. Will grabbed it, dropped the food on it and held it out to her.

'Thank you,' she said, taking out her small eating knife, before looking up.

'My name is Elizabeth Farrell,' she whispered.

He nodded, and, raising his scalded hand to his mouth, tasted the soup on his fingers.

2

Clutching two sets of reins in her hand, Elizabeth looked at the castle of St Briavels. The yellow-stoned walls glowed pink under the sunrise, and jagged shadows from the raised portcullis stretched across the path. Twin towers stood either side of the arched entrance, where the guards — armed with pikes — rested against the bricks. She breathed the fresh, cool morning air, and glanced back as her horse snorted.

'It's all right, girl,' she said, patting the animal's nose.

Narrowing her eyes, Elizabeth turned to stare back down the path. Where was Will? She didn't like the way the guards were watching her. It wasn't common for a woman to stand alone in the street, and she didn't want the men to come over and demand to know her business.

Footsteps echoed from the passage-way and Will stepped out into the sunshine. Her shoulders relaxed.

'I've arranged for passage to the nearest convent for you,' he said. 'Edmund won't find you there. Are you certain you wouldn't rather return home though?' He reached out and took the reins of his horse from her.

She remembered the betrothal con-tract and shook her head.

'You'll be safe with the nuns,' he said. 'They seemed a nice group, with a rather stern Mother Superior.' He grinned. 'She was quite intent on ensuring none of the younger woman came near me.'

Elizabeth smiled. 'Thank you for sorting out my travel. I'll send word to you when I reach safety.'

She looked away from his direct gaze, cheeks burning. It was wrong to lie, but she had no intention of joining the party riding to the convent. She'd had enough of being ordered around. As soon as Will rode back into the forest, she would hire a couple of servants and travel to her mother's land in the West Country.

Shifting on her feet, a clank of coins came from the two heavy bags she had tied around her waist. William had returned her small dowry so she could at least support herself until her mother's old farm was up and running. Shame there wasn't enough coin to pay off Edmund; but with luck, he'd get tired searching for her and marry someone else.

Will moved beside her and his arm brushed hers. The sudden warmth made her jump.

'You need to go,' she said. 'Your servants will be waiting and they shouldn't stay too long in the forest; I believe it's infested with outlaws.'

He laughed and looked at the trees. 'Get word to me if you have any trouble. My lands are at Shorecross, and a good messenger would find them.'

'Thank you for the help. You must

take back your mantle.' She raised her hands to the fastening at her neck.

'No, you keep it.'

He grasped her hand, and she took a step back at the sudden warmth. There were golden flecks in his dark eyes that she hadn't seen before. Will kissed her palm, his stubble rough against her skin; taking a deep breath, she pulled away.

'I must go,' she said.

He nodded, and Elizabeth curtseyed formally. Biting her lip, she watched him stride down the path and swing himself into the saddle. Already she missed him. As his dark horse vanished into the trees, she drew his mantle round her and breathed in his scent from the fur collar. Her horse neighed and she reached out to pat her, glancing again at the castle guards. Now Will had gone, she must be careful. Pressing her lips together, she glanced back down the path. Was travelling alone really a good idea?

No, it wasn't the time to have second

thoughts — not unless she wanted to end her days in a convent. She'd be fine once she reached the farm. She just had to find out where it was.

Laughter drifted over from the castle entrance and she turned to look. A group of women strode out through the arched doorway with baskets on their arms and skirts sweeping the floor. Watching them, she sighed, wishing it were her out shopping for her family. But Edmund's tyranny had taught her that marriage could be a dangerous occupation. As much as she wanted children and a home to call her own, if that place was filled with misery and fear, she'd be better off alone.

Remembering Edmund, she glanced into the forest. Where was he? It seemed likely he might head for St Briavels too, so she needed to move fast. First she would hire a couple of servants to accompany her — a man at arms and a maid, at least. It would be too dangerous to attempt the journey alone.

Holding the reins of her horse, she walked through the long gatehouse of St Briavels castle. Footsteps echoed behind her, and she twisted her head around to look. Was it Will? No, just a boy leading a mare.

Moving sideways, she let the child past, following him into the castle courtyard. Wrinkling her nose, she stepped over a layer of straw matted with horse dung which covered the cobblestones. Dozens of stalls had been set up in the castle grounds, piled high with fabric bolts, baskets of bread and heaps of turnips. Already men and women clustered around the tables, yanking out the cloth to drape in the mud and squeezing the apples. The sweet scent of over-ripe fruit mingled with sharp sweat and earthy manure.

'Fresh bread, mistress?' a market stallholder shouted.

'No, thank you,' she said.

She couldn't have swallowed food any more than eaten the reeking straw beneath her feet. A lump, painful and hard, blocked her throat. The warm smell of spice drifted again from Will's fur cape, and she pushed the mantle back, striding towards the hiring platform. William Downes had gone and she would never see him again. A sharp point hit her foot and she looked down at a hen pecking the soft leather of her shoes. Smiling, she pushed it away. The plump bird reminded her of her uncle's farm; taking a deep breath, she closed her eyes. How she wished she could feel his comforting arm about her shoulders. He would have been horrified if he knew how Edmund had treated her, but because she loved her uncle, she could not return home. The risk to him was too great.

Seeking comfort, she stroked her horse, the creature's emerging winter coat rough under her palm. Where would she be living by the time snow fell?

Then a hand grasped her shoulder, fingers biting deep. 'Greetings, my bride,' a male voice said.

Elizabeth froze.

Will trotted down the narrow forest track, his servants following on mules behind him, hooves quiet on the beaten earth. Occasionally he glanced at the empty space beside him.

'You're quiet, my lord,' Robert said. 'Not far now to Shorecross now. It'll be good to get back.'

'Yes, we've been away for a while.'

Usually on the journeys home, his thoughts were filled with Shorecross; today, however, he couldn't remove Elizabeth's face from his mind. Was she safe?

'I wonder if Edmund is still in the forest?' Robert said, ducking beneath a low branch.

'I hope so.' He pressed his lips together. 'Mistress Farrell will be in trouble if he finds her.'

'Could she not have come with us?'

'And what would we have done with her? You can't pick up a girl like you would a puppy.' Will sighed. 'The trip to find Edmund wasn't very successful. It's caused trouble for an innocent woman and warned Edmund that we are after him. We never should have searched for him while our blood was hot for revenge. It served no purpose and Joan must never know of it. Unbelievably, she loves him still.'

Robert moved his horse nearer. 'And her pregnancy? How can that be hidden?'

'We may have to adopt the baby out of the family, but that would break Joan's heart and she has suffered enough already.'

'And Shorecross would lose its only potential heir.' Robert shifted in his saddle. 'If Edmund gets control of Shorecross on behalf of his son, there is no way I would stay on the estate, my lord. He is a monster.'

'At least you can leave. Many of my workers are villeins and tied to the estate.' Will's grip tightened on the reins. How could he hide the child?

Elizabeth's face drifted back into his

mind, and his eyes narrowed.

'My lord?' Robert said.

Will turned his horse in a fast circle.

*   *   *

'I'll never marry you!' Elizabeth said, twisting under Edmund's grip.

'I have our marriage licence and there's a church outside the castle,' he said.

She glanced at his servants, but they stared back with unfocused eyes. Edmund slapped her across the face, a heavy blow that knocked her to the filthy straw. She lay still, her cheek and mouth stinging.

'Hey!' a man said. 'What are you doing?'

She pulled herself up onto her knees. The man was a bearded castle guard, armed with a pike.

'She is my wife,' Edmund said. 'And a man is allowed to chastise his woman.'

'I'm not married to him,' Elizabeth

said, warm blood from her split lip flowing into her mouth. 'I beg you, please help me.'

Edmund took hold of her arm, pulling her up.

'Come with me, or I'll send your uncle to debtor's prison,' he whispered.

'Are you all right, mistress?' the guard said.

She looked at Edmund's set, cruel mouth. People died in debtor's prisons. Standing, she wiped her face with the edge of Will's mantle and lifted her chin.

'I'm fine, I slipped.'

The guard nodded and strode away.

'Sensible girl,' Edmund said.

'Just let me go. Wed me, and I'll spend every waking hour making your life a misery.'

'And I'll apply the appropriate punishment, as the law allows me to.' He grasped her arm. 'Bring her horse,' he said to his servants.

Pulling her through the gatehouse, he dragged her onto the mud path outside the castle. Opposite lay a small church with a walled graveyard, an open front door and bell tolling in the tower. Tall trees overshadowed the roof, casting dark shadows over the stained-glass windows. Elizabeth's stomach clenched and nausea rose in her throat. He was going to force her to marry him? She couldn't wed this man! Desperately, she tried to pull herself free.

'But a priest won't marry us on your say-so!' she cried.

'Well, he agreed to last night, when I explained I had a licence.'

Elizabeth drove her elbow into his chest and he gasped, releasing his hold, then grabbed her shoulder and held it tight, his foul breath filling her mouth.

'Think of your uncle, starving and shackled,' he said, 'all due to the disobedient niece he treated like a daughter.'

'It won't be my fault, it's yours! You are a truly evil man.'

'And I can be worse, so obey me like a good wife should.'

Dragging her through the graveyard, he pushed her through the church door. Inside, an empty standing space led up to an altar where black and red paintings of agonised faces stared down from the walls.

'Why?' she said. 'Why do you want to marry me? I have nothing!'

'You have land.'

'But it's worthless.'

He looked down at her. 'Sign it over to me and I'll let you go.'

'It's all my mother left me.'

'You'll lose it anyway, as soon as we are wed.' He yanked her up the aisle. 'We are here to marry!' he called, looking around the church.

A priest stepped out of the chancel wearing a long dark robe and looking at her, he frowned.

'Why is she covered in blood?'

'A riding accident, but she's well enough to wed. I guarantee that.'

Elizabeth stared at the man; she couldn't marry Edmund, not even to save her mother's lands.

'You can have the fields, if they mean so much,' she said, 'but you will not have me.'

The door to the church banged and a man shouted, 'Why do you need to give him your land?'

She stared down the aisle, mouth open. Will stood in the nave, muscles tensed and a hand on his sword. He looked at her and his lips pressed together in a white line.

'You'll pay for this, Edmund. Each injury you have inflicted will be returned to you tenfold, until you are lying in the gutter screaming for mercy.'

'No weapons will be drawn in this church!' the priest shouted. 'Have you no shame?'

Edmund stared at the sword. 'If she gives me her land, I'll break the betrothal contract. I don't want her anyway, she's a bloody nuisance.'

'What contract?' Will said.

'I signed a betrothal agreement,' Elizabeth said. 'If it's broken, I have to pay compensation.'

'Then I'll pay it,' Will said.

'No,' Edmund said. 'She promised me the land.'

'I know the law, Edmund, and you can't refuse to accept the money. I'll send it to your lawyers. Inform them the contract is broken, and you'll have no further recourse.'

He held out a hand.

'Elizabeth, come here.'

She jerked free from Edmund's loosened hand and ran down the aisle. Will took her arm and leaned down.

'I'm alone,' he whispered. 'Edmund has servants outside and we must flee. I saw your horse tied to the railings, so come quick. We must get mounted.'

'Stop!' Edmund shouted.

'Come, Elizabeth!' Will gripped her arm, pulling her towards the door.

Elizabeth ran, her skirts tangling around her legs. The church door was open, and outside, two horses waited. Will boosted her up, then swung himself into his own saddle. Flicking the reins, she thundered up the pathway.

'Stop!' Edmund screamed from the church door.

Gripping her horse tight with her legs, face throbbing and lungs aching, she raced away.

A mile up the road, her mare trembling beneath her, she looked back. The path was empty.

'We can slow down now. You don't want to fall off again,' Will said.

She drew in her panting mount, trotting her through trees. Roots stuck from the floor and the path narrowed, shadows playing over her arms as the canopy thickened above. Birds sang and ferns rustled.

Will stopped. 'We've lost him,' he said. 'Robert's waiting with the others ahead. I thought we'd make a quicker escape with just the two of us.'

'You came back for me.'

'You were supposed to be travelling to a convent with a group of nuns. What were you doing in a church with Edmund?'

'Look at the state of me!' She pointed

to her battered face. 'Do you think I had a choice?'

'Why didn't you tell me about the betrothal contract? I'd have paid the compensation.'

'But I don't know you! How could I have asked you to pay? Don't be foolish.'

'I'm paying it now.'

'Yes, and why are you paying it? What do you want from me?'

He tightened his grip on the reins. 'I need your help.'

She pressed her lips together. 'I had a feeling this wasn't purely altruistic. What do you want?' She gave a short laugh. 'As long as it doesn't involve weddings, I'll consider it.'

'Will you marry me?'

'What?' She stared at him, mouth open.

'I need a wife so I can save my sister from disgrace and give my land an heir.'

'Then why not adopt the child? It isn't unusual for an uncle to raise his sibling's children.'

'Because if Edmund finds out Joan has had a child, he will try to claim the land on my death. I must have a wife to pass off as the child's mother.'

'I'm not going to take another woman's baby! Do you think I am heartless?'

'I think you are desperate. And I am not giving away my niece or nephew. All I need is a wife to live with me for a few months, to convince people that the child is mine rather than Joan's. You can leave as soon Edmund has been dealt with, and we will claim an annulment.'

'We can't claim 'lack of consummation' if there is a child!'

'There are other grounds.' He looked at her. 'I would never touch you, though: the marriage would be in name only.'

She backed her horse away. 'I can't marry you, not after what Edmund did to me. A husband has too much control.'

'There is no danger of being tied to

me. I can assure you of that.'

She looked at him. His chest rose and fell rapidly, and his knuckles were white from gripping tight on the reins.

'I'd sign your land back to you,' he said. 'And it would protect you from Edmund. He wouldn't dare come to Shorecross, we are too well guarded.'

'I do not wish to wed, though.' Helplessly, she dropped her head. It sounded so reasonable, but their union would remain unconsummated only as long as he wished it to be. He was a lord, legally in charge of his men, household and wife.

'I haven't laid a hand on you yet,' he said. 'And there was ample opportunity.'

'Neither did Edmund at first.' She looked at him. 'Do I have to decide now?'

'Yes, else I will have to ask a woman from the village. I would rather you though; you were raised a lady and would be an appropriate bride for me to take. As eager as my mother is for me to marry, even she would balk at a serving wench.'

'I would rather be a serving wench than wed.'

'Try it. You'll soon find the life has little to recommend it. Believe me, it would be easier to live at Shorecross than spend your days scrubbing vomit off flagstones and squirming away from grabbing hands. You wouldn't last an afternoon. If you won't marry me, then you must go back home or to a convent. There is nowhere else you would be safe.'

'I cannot go home, Edmund would find me there. I'm intending to go to my lands in the West Country.'

'To starve over winter? Don't be a fool.'

'You've no right to speak to me like that! I'm not a fool for not wanting to marry a man I have only just met.'

His mouth quirked upwards. 'True, but it will not be a real marriage, and I'm not a tyrant. You'll be well cared for, amply rewarded, then sent off to your lands in the spring with an escort and my thanks.'

She hesitated. Will was right; with winter approaching, it was no time to make a living from a neglected farm.

'All right, I will come with you. I won't sign another engagement contract though. Until the day of the wedding, I reserve the right to change my mind.'

He nodded. 'We'll marry at my estate, Shorecross. It will need to be soon, if we're going to convince people that a child already conceived is a product of our marriage.'

'Do I have to wear a shawl tied around my stomach?'

He laughed. 'We have so few visitors I doubt anyone would notice. You can always hide in the solar later.'

Elizabeth nodded and reached up to touch her face, dried blood peeling off under her fingertips. Will leant forward and cupped her jaw.

'I'll remember these bruises for when I next meet Edmund,' he said.

She shivered as his warm, strong hands held her chin; her mouth dry. Tracing his finger down, he smoothed it over her neck. She pulled away.

'I thought you weren't going to touch me?'

'My apologies, mistress; it won't happen again.' He straightened and flicked his reins. 'If we ride fast, we'll reach Shore-cross tomorrow night, where I'll be able to pass you into the care of my mother.'

'You'll pass me nowhere. I'm not your true wife and you'll have no say over me.'

He grinned and trotted down the path, leaving her to follow.

3

Elizabeth's riding habit tightened across her chest and she hastily signalled her horse to stop. A long bramble had snagged on the woollen fabric — she'd drifted too close to the hedge again. Pulling the thorny branch off, she sucked her finger as a bead of blood appeared. Jagged brown leaves drifted down from the trees above, casting moving shadows over the narrow lane; squeezing her legs, she indicated for the animal to trudge forward.

The mare moved into a slow walk and Elizabeth patted its neck. If Will didn't call a halt soon, she would. Thick clay mud reached above the animal's fetlocks, and the horse trembled as a powerful blast of icy wind blew down the red scarf her rider wore as a hood. Reaching up to the soaked wool, Elizabeth squeezed out a stream of red water, which stained the edges of Will's fur cloak a pale pink. She rubbed the mark surreptitiously. Would he notice?

Ahead, he reined in his horse and looked back.

'We're nearly there, Elizabeth!' He had tied his drenched hair back at the nape of his neck, and the sleeves of his doublet clung heavily to his arms.

'Please take your mantle back,' she said.

He shook his head and grinned. 'This is Shorecross weather.'

The path ended at the next corner and, shielding her eyes from the rain, Elizabeth stared at a tall, grey, stone curtain wall set with a black iron portcullis. Two men stood behind the gate with their pikes raised and she shrank back, palms sweating. She had expected a farm like her uncle's, not a fortified manor house. She glanced at Will. In truth, she hardly knew him. What if his intentions were not honourable?

Will swung down from his horse to

approach the portcullis and her shoulders relaxed as the guards grinned, bowed and opened the gate. A loud clunk echoed down the lane, followed by a squeak and rattle as the heavy iron barrier rose into the air. Noticing sharp metal teeth along the base, she touched the back of her neck with a shiver.

'It's only locked because I wasn't at home,' said Will. 'Shorecross isn't a prison and you'll be free to wander as you wish.' He put a hand on her bridle to steady her mare. 'My sister and mother are expecting you. The messenger was instructed to tell them you are to be my new bride.'

She shivered and looked away.

'Don't be alarmed,' he said. 'I don't wish to be wed either.'

'Are you going to tell your family the plan?' she said.

He shook his head. 'My mother is an honest woman and wouldn't approve.'

'Which implies I am not honest?'

'We're similar, and lie when it is vital we do so.' He grinned, then glanced into the trees behind her.

'Do you believe Edmund has followed us?'

'He knows where Shorecross is.'

A twig snapped in the bushes and she tensed. The gates to Shorecross looked more inviting now. Wrapping his reins around his hand, Will strode through the arch, and Elizabeth trotted her mount after. She wouldn't dismount until she knew it was safe.

Halting her horse in the courtyard, she breathed in the scent of roasting lamb and sage. It came from an outdoor kitchen: the open door revealed a brazier of leaping flames and a man lifting a rack of manchet bread from the oven on the wall. Her stomach rumbled; it had been a long time since lunch.

Behind the kitchen stretched the long front wall of the manor house, forming one side of the courtyard, which had been filled with stable blocks and a large well. The house had a large double door, left open, and small, leaded windows, which glowed under the pale autumn light like dozens of interested eyes.

'Let me take your reins,' Will said, striding towards her.

She hesitated.

'Unless you would like to sleep in the stables?' he said. 'I do not allow horses into the bedchambers.'

Looking behind her at the armed men, she gathered her reins into one hand and passed them to him. It would make no difference if she were mounted. An arrow could just as easily go through her back. She let him help her down.

Footsteps thudded across the mud, and she turned to see a man, wearing the doublet and hose of an upper servant, run towards them, then stop and bow.

'I'm glad you've returned safe, my lord,' he said, glancing at Elizabeth. 'The ladies are on their way down.'

Elizabeth straightened her hood and reached down to brush dust from her skirts. What would they think of her, travelling without a woman? Her aunt would have called her a hussy.

Will stepped closer and whispered, 'There is no need to look so pale — you will be made welcome.'

Two women came out of the manor house and crossed the yard towards them. Although over twenty years apart in age, they were dressed identically in dark woollen gowns with plain linen coifs on their heads. Elizabeth's gaze dropped to the younger girl, and she drew a sharp breath as she stared at the swollen stomach that pushed the dress high under her girdle. Raising her head again, she noticed the girl's deep brown hair and wide chestnut eyes. She glanced at Will, then back at Joan to compare them both. His sister had a more nervous smile.

'Remember, they believe us to be in love,' Will said.

'I'm not sure I could be that good an actor.'

'Ssh, now.'

Elizabeth smiled as the two reached

her, and curtseyed.

'My son,' the older woman said.

'So formal, Mother,' Will said. 'Are you both well?'

'We are fine. I received your letter.' She looked at Elizabeth. 'My new daughter?'

'I am Elizabeth Farrell,' she said.

His mother's grey hair had been tucked firmly under her head covering, above pale blue, narrow eyes. The lines running down to her set, firm mouth deepened as she glanced at the servants who accompanied them.

'Where are your women, Mistress Farrell?'

'You can call her Elizabeth,' Will said. 'And she has none. It does not matter, there's been no impropriety.'

'It is unusual to travel alone.'

'I did have companions, but we became separated during the journey,' Elizabeth said. If she was going to be here until spring, it would be good to start off the right way.

'Yes, they died. Very tragic,' Will said.

Elizabeth straightened her lips.

His mother sighed. 'Then I will arrange for one of our maids to sleep in your room with you. I am Dowager Lady Downes, but you may call me Margaret, and this is my daughter, Joan.'

'Mistress Farrell,' Joan said, dipping her knee.

Elizabeth copied her. 'Delighted to meet you both.'

'And I'm pleased to have a new companion,' Joan said, but she studied Elizabeth carefully.

'There's a meal set out in the hall,' Margaret said. 'Unless you would prefer to eat in the solar?'

Elizabeth breathed in the scent of roasting meat again. A quiet dinner would have been preferable, but it was important for the tenants and servants to know their master had returned.

'The hall would be perfect,' she said.

'I'll show you around,' Joan said, 'since my brother will need to discuss estate business. The land obsesses him, but I expect you have already noticed that.'

Elizabeth followed Joan across the muddy courtyard, shivering under the keen wind.

'Your decision to marry was very quick,' Joan said.

'Yes, it was.'

'I also had a short engagement.' She patted her stomach. 'My husband is away at present.'

Elizabeth nodded. Did her new sister-in-law truly believe Edmund would return?

'We have prepared the green room for you, as my brother instructed,' Joan said, leading the way into the manor house, their footsteps echoing from the wooden floorboards.

Elizabeth looked back through the door to where Will stood talking to his servants.

'You won't be apart for long,' Joan said, smiling. 'Your chamber has a door leading to his dressing room; although, until the ceremony, Mother has locked it and taken the key.'

'A connecting door?' Elizabeth blinked.

'Do not worry.' Joan smiled. 'Shore-cross is a large estate, and Mother cannot be everywhere!'

'Pardon?' Her mouth dropped open.

Joan looked amused, and Elizabeth closed her jaw, remembering Joan was not an innocent maid, but a pregnant and deserted wife. To distract herself, she looked at the hanging tapestries of dogs and horses covering the white-painted walls.

'Did your mother stitch these?' she said.

'No, they're ancient. This estate has been in our family for three hundred years.' Joan glanced around. 'As has most of our furniture. If you are marrying my brother for his money, then I can assure you we don't have that much.'

'I have no interest in his money.'

Joan bowed her head. 'I apologise, but we have had many girls turn up here, hoping to be made a lady. To date he has shown no interest in any of them, so it surprised us when he turned up with you.'

'Believe me, I was equally startled. I can assure you, though, I am not here to gain a title.'

Joan nodded and reached out to open a door. 'The Great Hall.'

Elizabeth stepped through. Rows of trestle tables had been set up — far too many for just the family. Either there were guests at Shorecross, or they ate in the old style with their servants and estate workers. She hoped it was the latter; it was the way her uncle ran his own lands. A large fire flickered in the grate, with clouds of smoke rising to mingle with the carved rafters, and rows of narrow leaded windows lined the walls, through which a feeble afternoon sun shone, casting lines across the floor.

'Is Shorecross run by a steward?' she said.

Joan shook her head. 'We have one,

but he only deals with the tenant farmers. William takes care of the land himself.'

'I'd like to assist him. I helped my uncle on his farm, as he had no sons. It would give me something to do.'

'He won't let you. When Mother fell ill, I had to call on my relative, Edmund, for advice on the sheep because I didn't know what to do. Edmund knows about sheep farming, as he's a wool merchant.' She smiled. 'I didn't expect to wed him, though!'

Elizabeth nodded. Edmund had promised to let her help run his farms — they'd laughed about her doing the dirty work — but of course he'd never had any intention of them working together. Although she didn't realise it, Joan had had a lucky escape.

★　★　★

Will rinsed his fingers in the bowl, then wiped them on the table cloth, before sitting back in his chair, Margaret and

Joan were either side of him; Elizabeth sat opposite him, her face pale and shadows under her eyes. He glanced at the platters placed on the table, beside jugs of claret wine, which glowed crimson under the flickering flames from the fire. With Elizabeth looking so lost, his appetite seemed to have deserted him. Had he taken advantage of her situation?

Tapping his fingers on the table, he looked at his estate workers, eating from their trestle tables at the other end of the hall. He had known these people all his life, and they needed his protection. His gaze fell on a new baby, born in his absence. He studied the tiny face wrapped in swaddling clothes, and his fingers tightened on his wine glass.

'Are you all right?' Elizabeth said, her voice low.

She was perceptive, certainly.

'I'm fine,' he said. 'Is your meal to your taste, mistress?'

Elizabeth put down her cup of broth. 'Delicious.'

He smiled. 'I don't like eel either, but we arrived with short notice. It'll be better tomorrow. Have you tried the lamb?' He cut several thin slices from the roast and put them on her plate.

'Thank you.' She lifted a piece to her mouth with her fingers.

He glanced at the bruise on her cheek and his knuckles whitened on the knife handle.

'When do you plan to wed?' Margaret said.

'As soon as we can arrange it,' he said.

Elizabeth jerked upright.

'Are your family travelling here for the ceremony, Elizabeth?' Margaret said.

She moistened her lips. 'My parents are dead, but I'll write to my uncle.'

'He'll be delighted to hear a date is set. Engagements can go on for such a long time, I wonder why the participants bother getting betrothed at all.'

'My uncle does not yet know.'

Margaret's mouth fell open. 'William,

you must write immediately! Did you not ask permission?'

'It all happened very quickly. There wasn't time to talk to her guardian, but since I'm not requesting a dowry, I expect he will agree.'

Elizabeth slammed her eating knife down. 'You do my uncle a disservice! He wouldn't marry me off to save money. He arranged my dowry and sent it with me — money you took.'

Will raised his hand. 'I apologise for the insult; it was poorly said and not meant.'

Margaret frowned. 'William, why would you take her money?'

'It was a misunderstanding,' he said, stiffly.

'I see little love between you both at present.'

Will groaned; his mother could be very astute. 'Mother, we are both tired. It has been a long trip.'

Elizabeth pushed her chair back.

'Music!' Joan said.

'What?' Will stared at his sister.

'Music. To celebrate your return. Minstrels, play for us.' She waved at them.

Will dropped his head into his hands. Joan had never been able to cope with confrontation — she had seen too much of it when their father was alive.

4

Edmund's legs trembled and he clung to the side of the courtroom box, then winced as cold iron manacles cut into his wrists. The connecting chains clanked and he stared at them, mouth open. How dare they arrest him as if he were a common criminal! Raising his head, he looked around the room for a friendly face, but his creditors in the viewing area gazed back through narrowed eyes.

The judge cleared his throat.

'You'll be held in the Fleet Prison until the debt is paid,' he said.

Edmund's fingers tightened on the woodwork. 'My lord, not there! I beg you. I'll die in those stinking cells. It was only a twelve pounds debt, and with my freedom, I could pay it in a week.'

'Yet you haven't paid it this past twelvemonth.'

'I forgot. I'm sorry. I'll pay it now.'

The man merely glanced at the guards standing behind Edmund and nodded.

'My lord, please!' Edmund said. 'There's been a mistake.'

'I don't believe so. Learn your lesson and pay those you have borrowed from. I see dozens of the likes of you in this court, men who think they can spend their way through life with other people's money. Stealing!' He brought his fist down on the desk. 'That's what I call it!'

'But . . . ' He stared at the man, nausea rising from his stomach. 'I'm a man of standing.'

'Then I'm sure there are friends who can bail you out. Take him away!'

Edmund grasped hold of the wooden sides of the box, splinters digging into his hands, as the guards tugged on his chains.

'Stop it, you bastards!'

'Come, sir, your cell awaits,' one of the guards said, grinning.

The chains pulled again and Edmund screamed as the metal dug into his hand, breaking the skin and sending a warm trickle down his wrist, staining the grey iron fetters crimson. He whimpered, but another tug on the chains pulled him from the box and to the door leading from the court. Looking over his shoulder, he stared at the lawyers sitting at their desks who had sat by smirking as he had been condemned, when any one of them could have saved him.

'Hurry up,' the guard said. 'We've dozens of your sort to deal with today.'

'Then take these damn chains off so I can walk.'

The man laughed. 'Step carefully down the steps, now; we wouldn't want you to trip.'

Edmund shuffled down the stone stairs, catching his shoulder on the wall as he stumbled. He would get William Downes back for this! If he'd had either Joan's dowry or Elizabeth's lands, he could have paid off his creditors.

'Faster!' the guard said. 'I've got a dozen to get to the Fleet this morning.'

Edmund climbed down the last stair stepped into a cellar room, dimly lit by tapers. The bricks glowed green with slimy mould, reflecting glints of light like the eyes of a frog. Rows of prisoners sat bound to each other on the filth-strewn floor — pitiful wretches in stinking rags with sharp, starving faces. Edmund dry-retched at the stench of vomit, sweat and excrement. Did he really have to stand beside these creatures?

The guards fastened him to an elderly man whose red-flecked rolling eyes pleaded for death, and whose cold, wrinkled hands — more like those of a corpse than a man — gripped his when they touched. Edward curled his fingers up. Goodness knew what diseases the creature had.

'Prisoners, walk!' a guard said.

The line of men rose to their feet, chains clunking and groans echoing around the small room. Edmund shuffled after, grimacing at each step. A clang of bolts echoed down the corridor, and he stepped through an open door into the familiar streets of London. The shouts of children mingled in the air with the yells of hawkers and a tantalising smell of fresh roasted pork filled his nostrils.

The shackles dug into his ankle and blood soaked into his hose. Cursing, he dragged his leg forward, causing the old man behind to stumble and cry out. With a slight twist to his lips, Edmund did it again. Then the amusement of tormenting the creature faded as a stench of rotting food and sewage filled the air, choking his lungs and coating the back of his throat so heavily he could taste it. It was an odour he had smelled many times before when he visited those he'd incarcerated for debts. It was the foul soup of the Fleet River.

'Through the gate!' a guard shouted.

It was the screams Edmund heard first: high-pitched, wolf-like howls as the inmates thrust impossibly thin arms through the alms grille, holding palms outstretched for coins. He moved too close, and the fingers, clawed and bloodied, grasped his clothing. He elbowed sharply down, striking them from his doublet. The gate slammed shut behind him.

Inside in the courtyard, the walls were high, and the ground beneath lay rank with puddles. A rat scurried around the yard, swollen fat and with glossy fur, until a hand emerged from a bundle of rags on the floor to grasp it. The creature squealed, biting, and the prisoner flung it away with a screech that sounded barely human.

'Stand in a line to have your shackles removed,' the guard shouted.

Edmund stood still, his wrists burning against the iron.

'Hands,' a guard said, stepping in front of him, holding a key.

Edmund held them up, fighting back an urge to weep as the man removed the manacles. He looked at his wrists, at their skin: red and broken as though he had thrust them into a fire.

'You're to see the governor,' the guard said, leaning down to unlock the leg shackles. 'Follow me.'

Edmund nodded, wincing as cramp flared up his leg. Cursing, he stumbled after the man across the courtyard and into one of the arched entrances leading into the prison.

★ ★ ★

The governor sat at a table with his stomach spilling out against the wood, warming his hands against a large fire burning in the grate. The smell of meat porridge hung in the air and Edmund's stomach rumbled.

'I can arrange a room on the master's side for you,' the governor said. 'How much money do you have?'

'None,' Edmund said. 'That's why I am here.'

'Then if you want to stay alive, I suggest you beg from your friends. A man of your background won't survive

70

a week on the common side.'

Edmund fingered a ring in his pocket. It was all they had left him with. He remembered the common-side cells from when he'd visited his own debtors. They had been icy cold and flooded, with black mould thick up the walls and no food given.

'What about asking your mother?' the governor said. 'In my experience, they always pay up.'

'She is dead; my father also.'

He thought of the door he had nailed shut, the plague sign painted on the outside. No-one would enter a marked house except gravediggers, and by then the bodies would have been too decomposed to be questioned.

'There must be *someone* . . . ' the governor said.

'Of course there is. I work in the London wool trade. I'm a powerful man.'

'We have many powerful men here. If you pay the fees, you can meet them. Else the beggars and vagrants will be your friends.'

Edmund slammed his hand down on the table, but the man took no interest. Smiling, the governor reached for a ledger, signalling that the meeting was over.

'Shame you have no wife,' he said.

Edmund went still. He had forgotten Joan. Now, she wouldn't leave him to rot in the Fleet, would she? He'd been nice to her as he waited for her large dowry to be paid.

'I'll need writing materials and the means to send a letter,' he said.

The governor looked up, eyes narrowing. 'Paper is expensive.'

Edmund took the gold ring from his pocket and slammed it onto the table. 'It's all I have.'

The governor picked it up, weighed it in an expert hand.

'It'll do for a few weeks,' he said.

'It's solid gold!'

'And this is the Fleet. Comfort costs here. Do you want your irons back on?'

Edmund looked down at the broken skin on his wrists and shuddered.

5

Joan opened the door to the bed chamber, standing back so Elizabeth could look inside. A young girl stood by the fireplace, wearing a plain but serviceable dress, a linen coif covering her hair. She straightened her shoulders.

'The fire's been made up,' Joan said, 'and if you need more wood, your maid will see to it.' She pointed to a chest. 'I've left you some gowns.'

Elizabeth stepped into the room. It was a fair-sized chamber for a guest — then she remembered she wasn't a visitor here, but the future mistress. A large four-poster bed stood in the centre beside a dark wood clothes chest. A small table and chair waited beside the fireplace. The shutters were closed and red light from the small fire flickered across their surface.

'It's nice,' Elizabeth said. 'I did bring a small box of coin with me. Do you know where it is?'

'William took it to the strongroom.' Joan patted the bed cover and turned to the door. 'Let me know if you need anything. Your maid's a willing girl, but not gifted with intelligence.'

Elizabeth glanced quickly at the young girl standing beside them, her skirt bunched anxiously into her hands.

'What is your name?' she said.

'Alice, miss. Shall I get you water for washing?' she said.

'Thank you. And I'd like a cup of warm mead, please.'

'Yes, miss. I'll be straight back.' Alice bobbed a curtsey and hurried out the door behind Joan.

Elizabeth walked around the room and paused by the open fireplace to warm her hands above the flames. A hard burst of rain drummed on the shutters.

'Do you have everything you need?' Will said, from the door.

'I am fine, thank you.'

'Good.' He glanced at her riding habit. 'Mother has asked the seamstress to measure you for two new dresses tomorrow.'

'I'll pay you back.'

'I'm going to meet your expenses while you're here. Tell the reeve what you need and he'll write a list.'

'I can write; my uncle taught me.' She glanced at the closed shutters. 'I'd like to ride out in the morning. What time is the dressmaker coming?'

'If you're an early riser, you could join me for the estate round.'

She nodded. 'What do you farm here?'

'Corn, beans and peas mostly, although the new sheep are doing well.'

'Are you fertilising the fields at the moment?'

'Yes.' He grinned. 'Can you smell it? Nothing like the contents of the midden for encouraging good grain.' He glanced behind him and stepped into the room, pulling the door shut.

'We'll have to set our wedding date soon if we are to convince people that Joan's baby is ours. Are you sure that you want to go ahead?'

She remembered Edmund's hands pulling at her hair.

'I have little choice.'

'You understand it will affect your reputation?'

She shrugged. 'I don't mind. After my experiences with Edmund, I have no wish to wed again.'

'You could stay here after the annulment.'

She smiled. 'While after an annulment it is usual for the children to stay with their father, it would look odd if the discharged wife did. And I have no wish to exceed my welcome. Thank you for the offer, but I must take care of myself.'

'As you wish. I'll send word to the Bishop for a marriage licence.' He bowed. 'I bid you goodnight.'

* * *

'Morning greetings, my lady.'

Elizabeth opened her eyes and sat up in bed. Alice stood in the doorway clutching a tray, which held a hunk of dark bread and a mug from which honey-scented steam rose.

'Thank you.' She climbed out, rubbing the goosebumps on her arms.

The fire was dead in the grate and Alice drew a sharp breath.

'Sorry, I forgot. I'll make it up now.'

'Don't worry.' Elizabeth pulled the cover off the bed and wrapped it over her shoulders. 'I have to be quick as the master is waiting for me.'

'You have plenty of time. Lord Downes said he would be delayed.' Alice leaned down. 'Someone's been stealing!'

'Well, it certainly wasn't me,' Elizabeth said.

Stretching, she scratched her hair and glanced down at the dried mud under her fingernails. Goodness she must look a mess after a week of travelling, especially given the lice-ridden hostels Edmund had chosen.

'Could you bring me a large bowl and two jugs of hot water, please? If the master is running late, I will bathe first,' she said.

'Certainly.' Alice bobbed and ran out the door.

A basin of cold water stood on the table; after rinsing her fingers in it, Elizabeth pulled up a stool beside the dead fireplace and broke off a piece of bread. Someone knocked at the door and she turned. Was it Will?

'Come in,' she said.

Alice strode in carrying a burning taper; kneeling on the rug in front of the grate, she lit the fire.

'You need to clear out some of the dead ashes first,' Elizabeth said. 'Else it will never take.'

Swallowing her mead, she went to the chest of clothes and pulled out the gowns Joan had lent her. One sage-green, a second claret, the third midnight blue. They were pretty, but had narrow woollen skirts, which weren't wide enough for her to mount a horse.

Sighing, she pulled out her damp red habit and held it up, staring at the thick mud stains. Wrinkling her nose, she sniffed. It even smelt damp. Draping the dress over a chair, she used a rough piece of cloth to rub at the marks.

'I'm sorry, my lady,' Alice said. 'I forgot it last night.'

'Don't worry, it'll only get covered again from today's ride. Is the hot water ready yet?'

'I'll go and ask Cook.'

Alice hurried off, her footsteps echoing down the stairs. Elizabeth smiled — it would have been easier to go down to the kitchen herself and fetch the jugs. She scrubbed at the dress and pushed the chair towards the fire for it to dry.

'I've got the water, my lady. I'll set it up by the fire,' Alice said. 'I've got drying sheets and washing cloths too. Lady Margaret instructed me on how to bathe a lady and wash her hair.'

'I can do that myself,' Elizabeth said. She pulled off her shift and stockings;

then, shivering, leant over to place a folded washing sheet into the base of the large bowl. Stepping into it, she poured hot water from the jug over her breasts and stomach, warming her chilled skin and casting away the goosebumps. Reaching for a cloth, she rubbed it against the hard soap and scrubbed her muddy legs.

'Shall I do your back?' Alice said.

'Thank you.' Elizabeth knelt down in the tray — she was a good foot taller than the maid — and winced as the girl scrubbed her back with the vigour of someone rubbing rosemary into lamb.

'Thank you,' she said. 'That's enough.'

Reaching up, she pulled the pins from her bun, and her heavy, dark-brown hair fell down her wet back. Alice stepped forward again, and Elizabeth reached quickly for the soap.

'I'll lather my own hair.' She still had bruises from Edmund. 'If you could rinse it for me?'

Alice poured the water over Elizabeth's face. Coughing, she reached out for a drying sheet and shivered — the maid had forgotten to warm the sheet by the fire. Throwing it around her shoulders, she sat on a stool beside a small fire and pulled her fingers through her hair.

'I'll comb it,' Alice said.

'I can do it.' She didn't want to end up bald. 'If you could clean the worst of the mud from my riding habit, as the master will be waiting for me.'

'He won't mind, not with you being his bride.' Alice smiled. 'We're all delighted. Never thought he'd marry again.'

'Again?' Elizabeth looked over her shoulder. 'Has he been wed before?'

Alice frowned. 'Not my business to gossip, sorry, my lady.' She bowed her head. 'I thought you knew.'

'Please tell me.'

The girl's face crumpled and Elizabeth turned away. There was no point in upsetting her maid further. But where was his wife?

★ ★ ★

Standing in the courtyard, Elizabeth stared at the thin layer of white frost that coated the mud like flour puffed onto bread rolls. Shivering, she reached up to pull her woollen hood over her hair, glancing up at the bright blue sky above.

Wearing dark hose tucked into boots and a matching doublet, Will stood with his back to her as he spoke to his stableman. Her gaze dropped to his bottom, encased in the tight leggings. Clearing her throat, she looked quickly away. The sooner this sham marriage was over, the better, as she was thinking of him more often than she should.

'Ready to ride?' he said.

Elizabeth turned to her horse.

'Did you sleep well?' he said, clasping his hands to hoist her into the saddle.

'I did.' She ignored his hand and climbing onto a step, swung herself up.

Will placed a hand on the bridle. 'Are you upset?'

Elizabeth stared ahead at the red sun rising over the fields, then glanced down at his concerned expression. What business was it of hers if he had already married? He was either a widower or the ceremony had been annulled.

'I am fine,' she said.

'Good.' He swung himself up into his own saddle and looked back over his shoulder. 'We'll check the ploughing first, then the sheep. I'm hoping for a good wool harvest this year, as prices are in our favour. The Flanders weavers are taking all we can supply.'

She cleared her throat. 'Did you deal with the stealing problem this morning?'

'It was only apples from the store-room.'

'Children, perhaps?'

'It's usually the adults. We've been through some bad times here, and my workers often hoard food. If they were high-value items, I'd take it further, but there's no need to be heavy-handed over stewing apples.'

She looked at his creased brow and

weary eyes. During the night, she'd woken thirsty and, whilst searching for a drink, noticed a candle still lit in his study. His workload must be heavy indeed if he had resorted to reading after the sun went down.

'You have a large estate to care for,' she said. 'Is business good?'

'Shorecross has only shown a profit these last three years. My father ran the estate into the ground — fields weren't planted, animals were left sick. I've had to build it all up.'

'Could your steward could take over some of the work? He looked a dependable man.'

'I prefer to deal with it myself,' he said, his voice hardening.

Elizabeth squeezed her legs, urging her mount forwards ahead of him. The sound of hooves came from behind her.

'My apologises, madam. I know can be unreasonable about Shorecross,' he said. 'Slow down, please.'

She reined in and waited, her face set.

'I grew up here,' he said. 'My father's duty was to care for the people, but instead he let them starve while he gambled away money that should have paid for their bread. I inherited a bankrupt estate, and we don't have enough savings to cover a bad harvest. I don't work for entertainment, it's because I have to.'

She nodded. 'You have many responsibilities.'

He steadied his horse, his gaze on hers, and she breathed deeply, fighting a powerful urge to reach out and touch him. An urge she had never felt with Edmund. Will let go of his reins with one hand and reached out; his fingertips brushed across her cheek, then slid down to her lips, stroking them softly.

He cleared his throat.

'We should ride.'

Elizabeth nodded, the cold, damp autumn air cooling the heat that had risen to her skin. Flicking the reins, she followed him along the strips of ridge-and-furrow farmland.

'Come and meet one of my villeins,' Will said.

He stopped by a row of wattle-and-daub cottages with thatched roofs that reached low towards the ground, and swung himself out the saddle. Elizabeth slid down quickly so he couldn't offer to lift her; she hadn't recovered from the last time he touched her.

Woven twig fencing surrounded the dwellings, enclosing a small garden where the tops of parsnips, leeks and onions peeked bright green through the dark ground. The door opened and a woman looked out, her back arched as she rubbed a swollen stomach. Clinging to her skirt was a small girl, and over her arm, a vegetable trough. When she saw them, she stopped and dipped.

'Hello, Marie, how are you?' Will said.

'Fine, my lord. My husband's by the main barn since they're winnowing today.'

Elizabeth smiled; it had been her job on her uncle's farm to watch the workers separating the wheat grain.

'It was a good harvest this year,' Will said. 'This is Mistress Farrell; she's seeing around the farm today.'

'Would you like to come in, my lady?' Marie said.

'If it doesn't delay your errands,' she said, glancing at the basket. It would be useful to see inside the cottages for when she farmed her own land.

'Give me your reins, I'll stay here,' Will said.

Inside the house, Elizabeth blinked and coughed as smoke tickled her throat. The windows were small and narrow, half-shuttered against the cold day. Beside the grate stood a basket of firewood, and the large bed had a straw mattress and several blankets. Above the brick fireplace, an iron pot hung over the flames.

'That food smells nice,' she said.

'Pottage, my lady. We eat our supper in the great hall, but midday we cook for ourselves.' Marie took the lid off the pot and stirred it.

A cry came from the corner of the room and Elizabeth jumped. In the shadows, she'd missed the baby in a wooden cradle, swaddled tight.

'Could I pick him up?' she said.

'It's a girl, and of course you can, mistress.'

Elizabeth picked up the child, noticing Marie's lack of fear at speaking to her. Will had a good relationship with his workers.

'Aren't you lovely?' she said, holding the child in the crook of her arm and looking down at the wide round eyes. The blanket moved as the child tried to free a tiny arm from the wrapping, so Elizabeth loosed it, and immediately the little fist grabbed her finger and held tight.

'I can see you like children, my lady,' Marie said.

'My cousins have several children, and I do love cuddling them.' She smiled as the baby grabbed her cloak. 'How many do you have?'

'Two, and this one's due in early

spring.' Marie touched her belly. 'We've not lost any.' She gave a proud smile.

'Very good.' Elizabeth coughed as thick smoke swirled around the room. Choking, she stepped back outside, still holding the baby.

'You have a new friend,' Will said, looking at the baby.

'Yes, I must return her.' She gave the child a last cuddle, enjoying the warmth of the tiny shape in her arms, before handing her back to Marie. 'You're lucky to get her back; a few more minutes and I would have been tempted to keep her.'

Marie laughed. 'After last night, my lady, I'd be tempted to let you.'

Elizabeth climbed back onto her horse, using a tree stump as a step. She turned to Will and saw him watching her from his horse with a strange expression of sadness and regret.

'You like children?' he said.

Elizabeth flicked her reins. 'Everyone loves babies, don't they?'

He didn't answer, trotting his horse

faster down the field.

Shielding her eyes from the rising sun, Elizabeth looked across the well-tended fields and remembered her own deserted land. With poor soil, it would be hard to grow crops there. She climbed down from her horse and stood to watch the late winter sunrise over the fertile fields of Shorecross. Will turned his horse around and stopped beside her.

'Why did Edmund want my land so much?' she said, frowning.

Will climbed down, winding the reins around his hand. 'I'll write to my lawyers in London and ask them to get prices for your plot. It's strange he was so insistent about owning it.'

'I hear coal is becoming valuable. Could he have wanted it for quarrying?'

'I don't think there's coal in that area. But you've got the right idea — there's something on the land that he wanted.'

Elizabeth looked around at the long fields stretching into the distance.

'Do you have time to do that?' she said.

'I've always got time for Edmund,' Will said. 'He ruined my sister and broke several of my ribs, which have taken an annoyingly long time to heal. Edmund is a stain on the earth and we'll only be safe once he is dead or imprisoned.'

'He is also very clever, and when he hears we are to wed, he'll be after revenge.' She moistened her lips.

'Then let him come to Shorecross.'

Elizabeth looked at him, staring across the fields, his expression set and grim. The kindness he had shown to her, the consideration for his workers, had made her forget that he was a lord of the manor — granted power by the king to defend his family and people.

He turned to face her. 'Before we marry, I have to ask if there is any reason Edmund might believe a child of yours could belong to him?'

She gasped. 'No, there is no reason. He did come to my chamber, but I screamed and ordered him out.'

Will touched her arm. 'There is no need to fear that happening here.'

She nodded and impulsively placed her hand on his. But he quickly turned his palm, grasping her with a calloused hand that knew the feel of the soil and the weight of a sword. Elizabeth looked up, startled, but caught his gaze and froze, looking into his eyes, unable to turn her head away. Leaning down, so his breath danced across her cheek, Will brushed her lips with his own, then drew back and smiled.

'I think that will convince the doubters,' he said.

She looked around quickly. Margaret and Joan were watching from the entrance to the manor house. Hurriedly, she stepped back. Had they been there when he first pulled her close?

'Time for hot bread and cool ale,' he said. 'Let me help you mount.'

'No, I can manage.' She turned to her horse.

6

Edmund huddled in the entrance of the army tent and stared at the canvas walls vibrating from the pounding rain. In the practice field, a drill sergeant yelled, and the ground echoed with the distant boom from the cannon teams practicing on the hill. Shivering, he pulled his soaked shirt away from his skin and grimaced. A long ride to the Scottish borders late in the season didn't suit a town dweller, but with a price on his head, he had no choice.

He stared at the rugs on the tent floor, the glowing brazier, desk and narrow bed. Henry Percy's campaign tent contained more luxury than many houses. How he would like to see the arrogant young man begging for bread in the Fleet. Lips pressed tight, he looked down at the ring of pale, healing skin around his wrist, then turned his hand to stare at the festering purple wound on the back. With a shudder, he remembered the relentless hunger, mouldy walls and rats. Thank goodness Joan had sent him enough money to bribe his guard.

'Edmund. You wanted to see me?'

Henry Percy, son of the earl of Northumberland, strode into the tent, clad in his padded gambeson stained with sweat and rust marks from his armour. Edmund rose to his feet and sniffed. Not only was the man late, but he stank like a horse.

'I hear you're looking for men and soldiers?' Edmund said.

'Yes.' Henry Percy's lip curled. 'Are you volunteering?'

'My relative, Lord Downes, wants to join you.'

'Lord Downes? He fought under my father. Brave man, but a risk-taker. How many men can he raise?'

'Over a hundred, and if you send word he could be in Scotland at the end of the month.'

Henry nodded and strode to the desk, dipped a quill in the ink and started to write.

'You'll need to seal the letter, my lord, so he knows it's genuine,' Edmund said.

The other man raised his eyebrows and reached for a block of wax. Melting it over a candle he stamped hard with his signet ring, tilting the folded paper so Edmund could see the mark of the Earl of Northumberland.

'It will go under my father's seal.'

He looked pointedly at the doorway and Edmund rose reluctantly to his feet. He caught his feet on a rug and kicked it back down as if it were one of his dogs. How he loathed Henry Percy. What did it matter if he suspected something? Desperate for men, he wasn't going to question Edmund's motives.

Once outside the tent, he wrapped his mantle close, squinting up into the grey sky. In the south of England, the sun still shone with warming rays, but here in the high north, the frost lay in scattered patches in the grass. Rubbing his chilled hands, he breathed in a rich meaty scent and his mouth watered. Checking his pocket, he found three coins — enough for a bowl of stew. After the meal, he'd raid a few packhorses to fund his journey back to the Midlands, where he might even pass William Downes as he trotted obediently off on his fool's errand.

★　★　★

Elizabeth wiped a clear spot on the misted window in the solar. Through the tiny gap, she made out oxen straining at the plough, heavy rain lashing their backs. In the courtyard beneath, a maid slipped while carrying water from the well, landing in the mud with a squeal. It was a shame she couldn't go down to help the girl, but Margaret had looked so shocked when she suggested going out earlier, it seemed better to stay inside.

Resting her elbows on the window, she stared at the pale ball of the sun, willing for it to drop so she could go to dinner. Not because she was hungry, but for something to do. A bang echoed from the room behind her, and she turned. Joan was piling more wood on the fire, then hastily sat back down, a hand across her mouth.

'Alice, could you fetch Lady Joan a ginger tea?' Elizabeth said.

'Yes, my lady,' the maid said.

'I am all right. Just a little tired,' Joan said.

'You're shivering.' Elizabeth picked a green woollen blanket from the chest.

'I wish my husband were here to care for me.'

Elizabeth nodded, tucking the rug around her. It was hard to imagine Edmund taking care of anyone.

'I fear he has deserted me,' Joan whispered. 'I have only received one letter from him. Mother insists he is not coming back, and I am starting to suspect she is right.'

'He doesn't sound worthy of your love.'

Her future sister-in-law touched her belly. 'William said we are to pretend the child is yours?'

Elizabeth took her hand. 'Your wedding cannot be proved, and a child born out of wedlock isn't able to inherit.'

'Surely your own children should get Shorecross?' Joan frowned. 'My brother cannot mean to stop his own inheriting.'

'Not everyone is so lucky as to be blessed with children.'

'That is true. His firstborn did not survive.'

Elizabeth froze. 'Firstborn?'

Joan blinked. 'I beg pardon. I spoke out of turn.'

Frustrated, Elizabeth stood up and went to the fire, bashing the poker hard against the grate.

'Are you all right?' Joan said.

'Yes. Chilly.'

'I expect it is nerves since it is less than a week until your wedding. I was the same before I married Edmund.'

Elizabeth looked at her. 'You deserve better than him, believe me.'

'I love him.' She smiled. 'My brother is besotted with you; I saw him watching you last night across the table.'

Elizabeth inhaled sharply, but there was a tread of footsteps on the stairs and Margaret strode in. Behind her came a woman carrying a basket of pins and tapes, followed by Alice with a tray. The warm scent of ginger filled the room.

'Your dresses are ready for their final fitting, Elizabeth,' Margaret said. 'Though most girls turn up at their future home with a trousseau.'

'I brought a riding habit and a horse,' Elizabeth said.

'You'll need a wedding dress too,' Joan said.

'One of my new gowns will do.'

Joan shook her head. 'You can't wed in wool. What about the dress Aunt Mary gave me, Mother? It's perfect for a marriage ceremony. We'd have to let down the hem.' She looked Elizabeth up and down.

'That was intended for your own nuptials,' Margaret said.

Joan snorted. 'I think you'll be waiting a long time before I get a proper ceremony. But it is a wonderful dress and should be worn. Please borrow it, Elizabeth.'

'I would love to. Thank you, Joan.'

She didn't care what she wore, but it would avoid spending money and annoying Margaret further.

'I'll fetch the dress,' Joan said.

'Let me help you take off your gown, Elizabeth,' the seamstress said. 'So we can fit your wedding gown.'

Elizabeth glanced at her mother-in-law, but the seamstress tugged on her laces of her dress, pulling it down and leaving her red-faced in only her chemise.

'Here it is,' Joan said, walking back in.

'It's beautiful,' Elizabeth said, reaching forward to touch the pale-grey silk bodice which reflected the yellow firelight. Stitched down each side of the skirt were gold panels, and the neckline crossed to form a decorative fold.

'I'll unfasten your headdress. Brides can wear their hair loose,' the seamstress said, reaching for Elizabeth's hairnet.

Joan held out the dress. 'Try it on.'

Elizabeth slid her arms into the long, wide sleeves, the fabric cool against her skin, then breathed in deep as the tight bodice clenched around her waist. Aunt Mary must have been a slim woman. Hopefully, the dress would stay on with a strongly-fastened girdle.

'Stand on the stool so we can get the hem right,' the seamstress said.

Elizabeth climbed up, her hair falling loose to her waist; pushing it back, she jumped. Will stood in the doorway, staring at her.

'Do you like the gown, brother?' Joan said.

He cleared his throat. 'It looks well enough.' His brow creased.

Elizabeth stared at the floor. It was embarrassing to be caught in a wedding gown when she had protested so much about marrying. Stepping from the stool, she grasped the fine lace bodice and wrenched at it, forgetting in her haste that it fastened down her back.

'Let me do it,' Margaret said. 'What do you want, William?'

'I've received summons from the Earl of Northumberland. I'm to leave for Scotland in a week.'

'What?' Joan said. 'Why does he ask you?'

'I have no idea. He's requested men.'

'For battle? But Shorecross men are not trained soldiers.'

'I know. I will hire mercenaries.'

'So you intend to go?' Margaret said.

'I have no choice. It would be like refusing a summons from the king.' He looked at Elizabeth. 'We'll wed before I leave.'

She kept her eyes to the ground and gave a tiny nod.

'I am sorry to have interrupted.' He

bowed. 'I'll leave you to your work, ladies.'

Closing the door, Will strode down the passageway. He should have told Elizabeth that she looked lovely, but with her hair loose and her body wrapped in the gown of gold and silver, she looked so different it had unnerved him.

Irritated, he kicked open his study door and flung himself into his desk chair, staring at the ledgers piled on the table. Thrusting his hand forward, he sent them flying to the floor with a crash. For a brief moment he hated them and the responsibility they brought.

'I'm not sure that's going to help,' a voice said from the door.

'Mother.' He reached down to pick up the books. 'To what do I owe this pleasure?'

'I have suspicions Elizabeth is crying

in her chamber. And I don't actually blame her.'

'I'll make amends.'

Margaret slammed the door shut behind her and stood in front of him, her mouth set.

'I wasn't sure about her at the start. She arrived alone and with no dowry, but I think she's a good choice of bride. She'll stand up to you.'

'I know her virtues, Mother, that's why I'm marrying her.'

'But it was all so sudden. You have declared for years that you would never wed again.'

'It's my business.'

Impatiently, he looked out of the window at the yardland, peaceful under the autumn sky. How much better to be out there, dealing with things he understood. Away from women, battlefields and mercenaries.

'Must you go to Scotland?' Margaret said.

'Yes, unless I wish to forfeit my lands. Elizabeth and I will marry before I go.'

'Take your time. I think she suits you, but you didn't look too pleased to see her in a wedding gown. If you're having doubts, you must tell her. I had a terrible marriage, as you well know, and I wouldn't want my children to suffer the same fate.'

'I doubt Elizabeth is going to start drinking and gambling.'

'I don't want you both to be miserable.' Margaret turned to the door, but as she gripped the handle, she glanced back. 'William,' she added, her face lined and pale, 'you have to tell Elizabeth about Adela. Joan tells me she doesn't know.'

He nodded curtly, but when the door closed behind her, he dropped his head into his hands.

★ ★ ★

Elizabeth had pulled her door close, but not shut. Will raised his hand to knock but, realising it would give her the opportunity for her to refuse him, pushed it open. Elizabeth lay on the bed, her head against the pillows, eyes closed and hair bundled into its net.

'Are you well, Elizabeth?' he said.

'I am fine, my lord, just resting.'

'Since when have you addressed me so formally?'

He strode across to the bed and looked down at her reddened eyes and pale skin. Impulsively, he reached for her hand. The memory of Adela had disturbed him and he needed to be reassured that Elizabeth still lived. She drew a shuddering breath; leaning down, he kissed her hand, the soft skin trembling under his touch.

'You looked beautiful in your dress.'

'You didn't look pleased to see me in it.'

'I was regretting only our plan,' he said, his voice low. 'That you weren't really going to be my wife.'

Her hand pulled away.

'Don't be alarmed,' he said. 'I know you have no wish to marry. Even if I was able to, which I am not.'

'Why can't you?'

Will stared at her; he wanted to explain, for her to understand why he acted like he did, but his throat dried.

Elizabeth swallowed.

'You leave for Scotland soon,' she said. 'Let us marry before you go, to protect Shorecross. I can't bear the thought of Edmund here, treating Joan in the manner he did me.'

Will reached for her hand again and pressed his mouth to the smooth skin of her palm. She moved back, but smiled an impish grin, which made him suspect that if he were to reach over and unlace her gown, she would not object.

The clatter of oxen hooves in the courtyard outside reminded him of where he was.

'It's time for supper,' he said. 'I should change my doublet.' He looked down at his mud-covered working jacket.

Reaching into the pocket tied under his shirt, he pulled out a set of keys, and strode over to unlock the connecting door to his own room.

Elizabeth laughed. 'I thought your mother had taken the keys.'

'There are two sets. Here, keep it.'

Unhooking the key from the ring, he tossed it to her, and walked into his dressing room, leaving the door ajar. Pulling his doublet over his head, he unfastened the lacings on his long-sleeved shirt and slipped it off.

Taking clean garments from the chest, he glanced towards the door to her room. Elizabeth stood watching him through the gap in the doorway. Grinning, he tied the doublet up. It was lucky he hadn't changed his hose.

'Ready, my lady?' he said.

'I am,' she said, and a red flush stained her cheeks.

★ ★ ★

Elizabeth pushed her shawl back and glanced at the fire blazing in the great hall. Sweat beaded on her forehead and she took a mouthful of cool wine. The memory of Will stripped to the waist flooded into her mind, and she shifted uncomfortably on her chair. What would it be like to touch Will's smooth skin? She glanced at him, and looked hastily away as he looked back.

'How long will you be in Scotland for, William?' Margaret said, dipping her hands into the finger bowl.

'I don't know. Not long, I hope.' He frowned. 'It is a strange summons. The border lords usually deal with the Scots.'

'Is it worth checking?' Elizabeth said.

'It has the earl's seal. I am sure it is genuine, but I'll send a messenger to Northumberland to confirm.' He broke a piece of bread and put it down uneaten on his plate. 'I'll leave Robert here to protect you.'

'You'll need a right-hand man to help control the mercenaries,' Margaret said.

'I've managed them before, and the battle will likely be over before I get there.'

'But, William . . . '

'It is my decision.' He put down his knife.

Margaret looked down, twisting the tablecloth in her hands.

'I think we've finished eating,' Joan said. 'I do not wish for sweetmeats.'

Elizabeth put her untouched currant pastry on the table. The expression on Margaret's face frightened her. Will's hand brushed her leg under the table, and she pressed against him, breathing in his scent, so familiar and yet so disturbing.

'It's time to retire,' he said. 'It's late and we have a busy day tomorrow.'

Abruptly, he stood up, moving away from her touch. She turned away from him, but he touched her shoulder, looking down into her eyes.

'I will see you in the morning, mistress,' he said. 'Sleep well.'

★　★　★

A loud bang echoed through her room and Elizabeth jerked upright in bed.

'Who is it?' she demanded.

'It's only Alice and I,' Joan said. She flung back another shutter to let pale grey light flood into the room. 'Mother has arranged an early breakfast in the solar so we can discuss wedding plans.'

Elizabeth pushed down her sheets. 'I know nothing of weddings. I thought we only needed a priest?'

Joan laughed. 'You won't get away with that. Mother has booked minstrels and ordered a cow to be slaughtered.'

Elizabeth sighed. 'I wish we could wed as you did.'

'Your marriage will be legally binding,' Joan said. 'Mine is not.'

'My apologies; that was the wrong thing to say.'

Climbing out of bed, Elizabeth reached for her green day gown. It was tempting to tell Joan that her marriage wouldn't be legally binding either, but she'd promised Will she would say nothing. She hadn't expected this much fuss, though. Margaret and Joan's enthusiasm for the wedding would only make them despise her more when they discovered the truth.

'Mother is delighted about your marriage, even if she does not show it,' Joan said. 'After the disaster my own turned into, it is wonderful she can have something to celebrate at last.'

Elizabeth turned so Alice could fasten her dress. It would be cruel to dampen their enthusiasm.

'Come, then,' she said. 'Together we'll work out how many guests a cow can feed.'

* * *

Elizabeth squeezed around the large table in the solar, catching a jug of mead with her elbow.

'Do be careful,' Margaret said, snatching up a plate of currant pastries before the puddle of drink reached them. Throwing a piece of cloth over the spill, she went over to a basket of lace and silk fabric scraps standing by the fire.

'Fetch your silver dress, Joan,' she said. 'We need to add at least a foot of material onto the hem. Come and stand on the stool, Elizabeth, so we can measure you. The seamstress hasn't arrived yet and we can't wait any longer.'

'Could I have breakfast first?' she said, looking at the pastries.

'If you have too many of those, we'll have to widen the dress as well.'

'You'll have to widen mine anyway,' Joan said, walking back in with the dress and draping it over a chair by the fire.

'Not there! Use your senses, girl! It'll get covered in smuts.' Margaret snatched the gown.

Elizabeth hastily climbed onto the stool.

'Here,' Joan said, handing her a sweet bread roll.

Elizabeth clutched it with one hand, and hung onto the ledge of the fireplace with the other one, as Margaret measured her.

'Does William have a good robe — cleaned and pressed?' Joan said.

'I hope so, because we haven't time to make one. He'll probably turn up in a haymaking smock,' Margaret said.

'Mother! He wouldn't do that.'

'There's a very long list on the table there,' Elizabeth said, looking over their heads.

'Wedding guests,' Margaret said. 'Are there any names you want to add?'

Elizabeth shook her head. She couldn't bring her uncle all this way to witness a sham marriage.

Joan squeezed her arm. 'Don't worry, there was no one at my wedding either.'

'Well, there could have been,' her mother said, 'if you'd let us know you were being wed.'

'Edmund insisted on it being a private affair.'

'And that's not a mistake you'll make again, I'll warrant! Now, come with me, Joan. We have to find a dress that can be altered to fit you. People mustn't see you're with child, too many questions will be asked.'

Elizabeth stepped down and sat at the table, glad to be alone. Wearily, she glanced down the long list of names, but recognising none of them, threw it back on the table. Taking a mouthful of breakfast, she looked at her wedding dress again, and put down the sweet-meat as nausea rose from her stomach.

What was she doing marrying a man she hardly knew? Meeting his family had made her feel worse. They had accepted her into their home, and would be angry when they found out the truth.

Alice put her head around the door.

'You've got a visitor, my lady,' she said.

'Does the master know?'

Alice shook her head. 'The man says he's here to see you. He's on his way up now.'

Elizabeth went cold.

'Send word to Lord Downes to come urgently, and tell Lady Joan to stay in her chamber.' She couldn't risk the girl walking in, belly swollen under her gown.

Alice frowned, but nodded. Elizabeth took her eating knife from her pocket and pushed it up her sleeve, then crossing to the window, squinted across the fields. How far away was Will? Footsteps sounded outside the room and Alice held back the door.

'Your guest, my lady,' she said.

Elizabeth took a deep breath.

A bearded man walked into the room, clad in an old-fashioned black robe.

'That was a long journey!' he said. 'You really are in the middle of nowhere.'

'Uncle Walter! What on earth are you doing here?'

'When I receive word my niece is to marry, I like to come and meet the man concerned.' Her uncle held out his arms. 'My darling girl, it is wonderful you see you again. The house has been such a quiet place.'

She ran into his familiar and comforting embrace, but as she hugged him, a clatter came from the floor. Looking down, her eating knife lay spiked into the floor boards a few inches from her uncle's foot.

He stared at it, then the door flew back and Will stood in the entrance, sword held low.

'Goodness, you do take security seriously here,' Walter said.

'This is my uncle, Walter Farrell,' Elizabeth said quickly.

Will lowered the weapon and smiled.

'It's good to meet you, sir. I am Lord Downes.' Wiping his palm on his smock, he held his hand out to Walter, who grasped it firmly. 'I'll get changed and join you both.'

'Don't let me take you from your work,' Walter said. 'My niece can keep me company.'

Will bowed. 'I will see you at dinner then.' He went back out the door.

Elizabeth looked at her uncle.

'It is lovely you came for the

wedding,' she said. 'I hadn't expected it.'

'I was very surprised to receive your letter. What happened to Edmund?'

'He was not the person we thought.'

'So I have since heard. Two friends warned me after you left and I sent my men to find you, but his home was deserted. I was terrified until I got your letter. I thought he'd murdered you.'

'Lord Downes saved me and paid off my marriage contract. I am free.'

'I must pay him the money back, then.'

She shook her head, unable to explain that she had discharged the debt by agreeing to marry him. 'He doesn't even want my dowry.'

'Don't ever marry, Elizabeth, without paying the correct dowry, else eventually it will be held against you. That payment gives you honour and dignity. You're not a burden, but an asset.'

'He has the chest of coin.'

'Then I suggest you leave it with him.' He frowned. 'Are you happy, niece? This marriage is very quick, and I fear you do not understand his character.'

'Yes, I do.' Will's character was one of the few things she did know. It was his past that was unknown to her.

'Are you sure? Do you know that Lord Downes' father was a violent drunk who gambled away his family fortune? I have heard nothing but positive reports about William, but his family have a bad reputation.'

'He's already told me about his father, and that he has to work to make a success of the estate. Will is an honourable man, I'm sure of it.'

'The demon of thirst can take even honourable men.'

'In the evenings he has one glass of wine with supper, and during the day only watered mead or beer. I have never seen him drunk — I suspect he won't take the risk.'

'Is he violent?'

'No! He hasn't raised a hand to anyone while I've been here, not even to his servants. He's not the man his father was, I'm certain. I appreciate your caution, but he is a good man.'

'You have known him only a few weeks, and I have never met him before. If he turns to drink, to wife-beating, to affairs, you will still be married to him. There will be no escape for you.'

Elizabeth shivered and glanced at her wedding dress, draped over a chair by the fire. She moistened her lips.

'I'm sure it will be fine. Now, let me show you around the estate, as I think you'll be impressed. Will is more concerned about the welfare of his villeins then extracting the last ounce of sweat from them.'

'Then you've found a man with my own values. Your mother would be very proud of you.'

Elizabeth closed her eyes briefly and took his arm. There was no way her mother would be proud of her for marrying a man she hardly knew, with the purpose of deception at its heart.

* * *

Lifting the iron latch of the barn door, Elizabeth pushed it open and pointed to the sacks of wheat stacked high. The scent of dry grasses filled the air and motes of dust floated in the autumn sunlight.

'This is where we store the harvest.'

'That's a good amount you have collected,' Walter said. 'The fields missed your magic touch this harvest week.'

She smiled. 'I used to enjoy working with you; I don't have much to do here.'

'Then ask for a job. Lord William has a large sheep flock; you were always good at taking care of them. Though I expect you'll be too busy with babies soon to worry about the estate.' He smiled.

She nodded, tired of the pretence that she and Will would have a normal marriage. It was wrong to deceive her uncle, but she didn't have much choice.

Closing the barn door, she led him across the field.

'Let's rest for a minute,' he said, stopping by the trunk of a fallen tree.

She sat down beside him, the cold chill of the wood pressing through her woollen gown. Shielding her eyes with her hand, she gazed at the ploughed strips stretching into the distance, covered in the moving dots of woodpigeons who hopped between the furrows in search of worms.

'If you've any doubts about the wedding, I can take you home,' Walter said. 'I know you've never seen eye to eye with your aunt, but after Mary marries next month, I'm sure she'd appreciate your company.'

Elizabeth remembered her wasp-tongued aunt. It would take more than loneliness to make her civil.

'She is not so bad. Sharp-tempered, but not cruel,' Walter said.

'She resents me because I have been a burden in food and clothing.'

'You worked for your keep, many times over.'

Elizabeth looked across the fields. In the distance was a mounted man wearing a familiar mantle, and her chest tightened.

Walter pointed to the distant figure. 'Does he ever talk about his first wife?'

Elizabeth went still. 'What do you know of it?'

'Only that he wed at a young age to a girl called Adela, and was grief-stricken when she passed away.'

'Do you know how she died?'

He shook his head. 'I'm surprised he hasn't mentioned it.'

She bit her lip. 'We decided to marry so quickly, there was little time. I'm sure he will tell me when he's ready to.'

'It won't be an easy marriage if you have the ghost of a beloved wife between you.'

She sighed. In truth, there was nothing easy about this wedding. It was too late to change it, though. The guests would be arriving shortly. Will was a good and kind man, someone she would have been honoured to wed before she met Edmund. But the memory of how Edmund had changed into a violent bully stayed in her mind. If Will refused to annul the wedding, or if he attacked her on their wedding night, there would be nothing she could do about it. Could she trust this man?

★ ★ ★

Elizabeth put down her cup of morning mead and stared into the fire that Alice had lit early in her chamber. Even the warmed drink couldn't dissolve the tightness in her throat. Was she making a dreadful mistake in marrying today? Did protecting her uncle justify her lying to him? But now their guests had arrived — and the damn cow had been slaughtered — so it was too late to back out.

The door to her chamber was flung back and she jumped, spilling her mead.

'Good, you're up!' Margaret said.

'Greetings sister!' Joan said, smiling as she followed.

Elizabeth nodded, her stomach churning.

Joan stopped. 'Why so sad on your wedding day?'

'I expect she's nervous,' Margaret said.

Elizabeth cleared her throat. 'It's a little daunting.'

'There's nothing for you to worry about,' Margaret said. 'Did your aunt explain about your wedding night? What would be expected of you?'

'No, Mother, please!' Joan said. 'I'm sure Elizabeth knows.'

'That's all right, Lady Margaret,' Elizabeth said, quickly. 'My married cousin mentioned it a while ago.'

'It's not that difficult to work out, anyway,' Joan said, grinning. 'And while it's not pleasant, it doesn't last long, and then you can go back to your own room.'

'The less you talk about it, the

better!' Margaret said. 'And make sure you lace up tight. Your brother's been kind enough to save your reputation by taking on your child, so don't let anyone guess otherwise.'

Striding out the room, she slammed the door behind her.

'Mother still doesn't actually believe me that I'm married,' Joan said. 'Don't mind her today, she's got a lot to do. William invited dozens of people to the wedding, but forgot to arrange rooms or food for them. We haven't even enough tables in the great hall.'

Voices came from outside her window, so Elizabeth pushed back the shutters and looked out. A group of people were standing in the courtyard beneath, and waved up at her as she pushed her head out the window. Hastily, she pulled back into the room.

'I must help Margaret,' she said.

'Don't worry, Cook is taking out pitchers of ale to the new arrivals, and Robert's gone to the inn to hire extra trestle tables. You'll have enough to do today. Mother's just irritated because William's out in the fields instead of seeing to his guests. Although, since he is generally unsocial, I did tell her that he was best there.'

'I didn't realise he'd invited so many people.' She moistened her lips. It wasn't good to admit she had such little interest in her own wedding.

Joan grinned. 'After my disaster of a ceremony, I suppose my brother wanted to be sure there was no doubt over yours. I see the way he watches you.'

'I am sure you're mistaken.'

Joan frowned. 'It is a natural for him to look at his new bride with pleasure. I would only worry when he stops staring at you in that way.'

'Yes, that is true.'

Alice put her head around the door. 'The seamstress has arrived with your dress.'

Elizabeth took a deep breath and closed her eyes, excitement and fear spreading through her like the opening tail of a peacock. Would she regret this day? She was becoming too fond of Will when she was no more than a convenient bride.

'Elizabeth?' Joan said. 'It's time to get dressed!'

Elizabeth took a deep breath and turned, fixing a smile on her face. Their guests hadn't travelled miles on horseback to see a tearful bride.

7

'You look beautiful,' Margaret said, eyes shining with moisture. 'A perfect Lady of Shorecross. Much better than you do in that red habit you insist on wearing so often.'

'In Elizabeth's defence, she could hardly go riding in a wedding gown,' Joan said. 'But the dress does suit you so well. Aunt Mary would be delighted.'

Elizabeth looked down. The dress fitted close to her breasts and dipped in at her waist, the tight stays constricting her lungs. Behind her stretched a pearl-grey train, edged with gold lace.

'Is your Aunt Mary coming to the wedding?' she asked. 'I would like to thank her.'

'She died last year. The gown was left to me in her will,' Joan said.

Elizabeth smoothed the dress down, then pulled her hands away from the fabric. Was it a bad omen to marry in a dead person's dress? She glanced down at it again, then shook her head. What did it matter? It was unlikely Aunt Mary had actually been wearing the gown when she met her end.

'Sit down,' Joan said, holding up a comb and pins. 'I'll dress your hair. It would be cruel to inflict Alice on you today.'

Elizabeth sat on a stool and gripped the seat as her sister-in-law tugged off her hairnet. The long, dark strands dropped to her waist, and crackled with static as Joan pulled the comb through them.

'You've got nice hair,' she said. 'You can wear it down today as it's your wedding day. I've got some lovely pins mother has lent you. Do you like them?' Joan held one out.

Elizabeth touched the diamond clusters. 'They're beautiful.'

Margaret walked back into the room and Elizabeth glanced over her shoulder at her. 'Thank you for the pins.'

'I wore them on my own wedding day, as they were a gift from my father,' she said.

Elizabeth nodded as Joan pushed the pins in either side of her temples. Had Adela worn these same pins when she married Will?

'Finished,' Joan said, stepping back and putting a hand against her lower back.

'Thank you.' Elizabeth touched her hair, keeping her head straight.

'We should hurry,' Margaret said. 'William is waiting for you.' She handed Elizabeth a pair of slippers and glanced at her daughter.

'Fetch a mantle to go over that dress, Joan. We'll have to tell people you have a chill.'

'Then they will all avoid me.'

'Let's hope so.'

'Perhaps I should just sit in my room for the duration?'

'It would be questioned. You'll just have to lace up tight and wear a cloak.'

Elizabeth glanced at the high swell of

her soon-to-be sister-in-law's belly. 'Are you sure you are only six months?'

'I must be. He left shortly afterwards.'

'Hurry and fetch your mantle, Joan, else we will be late,' Margaret said. But she stood still, biting her lip, as her daughter ran out the door.

'Maybe it is twins?' Elizabeth said.

'Don't scare me, please! I've enough to worry about.' Margaret leaned down to straighten the hem of the wedding dress.

A knock echoed, and Walter put his head around the door. 'All ready?'

'Come in, Uncle,' Elizabeth said.

He smiled. 'You look beautiful. Your parents would have been so proud.'

Elizabeth looked down at her wedding dress and swallowed the lump in her throat.

Margaret reached over to squeeze her arm. 'Now, where are the flowers for your head?' she said.

'Robert brought in wheat stems.' Elizabeth pointed to the circlet of woven grasses. 'It's the wrong time of year for orange blossom.'

'With William's obsession over the land, it is quite an appropriate piece to wear.' Margaret picked up the head-dress and a pin. 'Lean down.'

She inclined her head, and winced as a sharp pin jabbed into her scalp.

'Ready?' Joan said, from the door.

Elizabeth swallowed.

*　*　*

Stepping through the iron gate behind her uncle, she stared at the grey stone walls of the church that stood outside the main courtyard. A few late-flowering irises flashed deep blue petals in the tangle of long grass edging the narrow mud path. The air was dry, warmed by the weak autumn sun that reflected from the polished upright gravestones, and filled with the sweet scent of drying hay from the fields. Distant voices, and the clop of hooves from a ploughing team at work, drifted from the farm.

Elizabeth knew that whenever she breathed in that scent again, it would bring her back to standing in her wedding gown, uncertain and scared. The day she married a man she'd only known a few weeks.

'Let me lift your train,' Joan said. She bent over, but straightened immediately and laughed. 'I can't. It's as if a hard cushion is tied to my stomach.'

'I'll manage,' Elizabeth said, and pulled her skirts close to her body, away from the thorns.

'Are you all right?' Walter said.

'Yes.' She took his arm, the sturdy warmth comforting.

People stood in groups outside the church. Will stood talking to his friend, but broke away when he noticed her walking down the path. She drew a sharp breath; he had dressed in a black and silver doublet, slashed at the arms to show a pure white lining, over matching hose and polished boots. It wasn't often she saw him clad as the

Lord of the Manor.

'You look lovely, Elizabeth,' he said, and held out his hand.

'Go to him, my dear,' Walter said.

Elizabeth gripped Will's fingers, the familiar roughness taking the chill from her own hands.

'Ready?' he said.

She nodded.

'Let's be wed, then,' he said.

She followed him to the church door and glanced back at Uncle Walter. He gave an encouraging grin and she smiled back, her shoulders relaxing. Of course it would be all right. Will was not Edmund, he would never try to force him attentions on her as the wool trader had. They would save Shorecross, then apply for an annulment.

Footsteps echoed from the dimly-lit church as the priest appeared at the door, clad in his long, dark robe. The man held out his hand.

'Licence, my lord?' he said.

'Here.' Will held it out.

'Thank you. Please come up to the chancel.'

Elizabeth held Will's arm and followed him into the building. Pale sunlight, coloured red and blue from the stained-glass windows, lay in patches on the stone floor. Bright murals depicting Biblical scenes, fiery red and unnerving, glowed from the wall behind the priest.

The priest stood in front of them and opened his book as two witnesses filed down the aisle. As was customary, most of the guests remained outside, chatting as they waited for the feasting to begin. Elizabeth jumped when the priest began to speak. He was using the same words as had been used for the betrothal ceremony to Edmund — only the tenses were different. Edmund had held her hand too that day, but the grip had been hard and cold. She closed her eyes to block out the sound of the priest's voice; it made the ceremony easier to bear.

'I now pronounce you man and wife,'

the priest said. 'And you can kiss your bride.'

Will raised her chin, and placed his lips on hers. Instinctively she parted her mouth and he did the same, kissing her deep and causing blood to pound in her temples.

Pulling away, she glanced at him and he grinned.

'Wife,' he said.

She smiled. He was a man she would have chosen as a husband — but it was vital that she guarded her feelings against him, or else she'd end up being hurt. This was a marriage of convenience and nothing more.

★   ★   ★

Elizabeth slumped in a chair and leant down to rub her aching feet. High-heeled slippers were not easy to dance in. It had been a marvellous day, though. Will's relatives and friends had welcomed her wholeheartedly. Straightening, she gazed up at the sweet grasses woven into the rafters, then at the long trestle tables pushed back and covered in platters of pork, chicken and swan. Baskets of bread and dishes of sweet-meats were still piled high, even though the guests had been feasting since mid-afternoon. The sweet scent of roasting suckling pig drifted through the open doors from the courtyard kitchen.

The floor vibrated beneath her feet from the beat of the music plucked by the minstrels. Sighing, she pulled her gown straight and looked through to crowd to spot Will. Host for the evening — she had barely seen him. After the church he'd been reserved, withdrawn almost. Was he remembering the last time he married? Had Adela sat in this hall with her stomach tight with nerves, waiting for her wedding night?

At least that wasn't something Elizabeth needed to worry about. Although they would share a room tonight, he had assured her that he would sleep on the floor. Tomorrow she would emerge from the room as innocent as she was today.

She glanced at where Will stood and smiled. He was directing the servants to place leftover food in baskets for the poor — even on his wedding day, her husband did his duty.

'Come and dance, Will,' Margaret called.

'Let us dance, then,' he said, taking Margaret's hand and whirling around to loud cheers.

Elizabeth's chest constricted, seeing his hair tousled from the heat, his doublet untied and linen shirt loosened to show a triangle of browned skin. A gentle hand touched her elbow. It was Joan, who had wrapped her cloak wrapped tight around her body, even though her skin gleamed with sweat. She hadn't danced much either.

'It's time to be retire to your chamber,' Joan said. 'But do not fear, Mother has told the other guests that they are not to accompany you. The priest has blessed your marriage bed.

He was generous with the holy water, so your union should be a fertile one.' She grinned.

Elizabeth turned to see her new husband striding towards her.

'We'll take our leave, Elizabeth' Will said, then raised his voice. 'Food and drink will be provided until dawn. Enjoy yourselves!'

'And you too,' a man shouted back.

He bowed.

Elizabeth followed him across the hall, cheeks warm. Lifting her gown, she followed him up the steps leading to the private rooms above the hall, but the candles hadn't been lit and she stumbled.

'Careful,' Will said, reaching back to steady her. 'Were you all right today? There was little time to talk.'

'Often the way in weddings,' Elizabeth said, looking at his hand on her arm and wishing it could remain there. She cleared her throat. 'I am weary tonight, my lord.'

'Then let's get you to bed.' He

turned back to the stairs and continued up to the landing.

A few candles had been lit at the top of the stairs, their tiny flames flickering beneath the tapestries that hung across the walls. From the hall beneath drifted the sounds of laughter and lutes, but on the landing there was only silence as she followed Will down the corridor to her room.

'I will join you soon,' she said, reaching for the handle. 'I understand that this night we must share the same chamber?'

Will took her hand from the iron latch. 'Come with me now.'

'I need Alice to help me with my gown.'

'I'll unfasten your dress.'

Her hand trembled.

He glanced back and smiled. 'You'll have sufficient layers of chemise underneath to avoid my touch. Come with me.' He strode to his own chamber then, opening the door, stepped back to allow her to enter.

Elizabeth walked in and stopped.

'My lord, it is beautiful,' she said.

A soft glow flooded the room from dozens of candles placed on the fireplace, the table, and clothes chest. The table had been set up with two drinking glasses which sparkled under the flickering flames. Beside them stood a tall wine jug and two dishes, one filled with blackberries and tiny apples and hazelnuts, the other with oatcakes soaked in honey.

She breathed in the scent of warm spiced wine and the fresh resin from new rush mats. Unable to resist, she turned to look at the bed, noticing it had been made up with a new silk cover, folded down to show clean white sheets. A cream chemise, with long sleeves and a delicate lace collar, had been draped across the pillows

'Did you do this?' she said.

'Except the chemise — that was Joan. She insisted you needed wedding nightwear.'

She flushed. 'It is lovely what you

have done, thank you. I was expecting an awkward night with you sleeping on the floor.'

'I wanted to show you that I appreciate what you have done. Shore-cross can claim an heir now without Edmund being involved.'

'Then today has served a good purpose.'

'Come and sit by the fire,' he said. 'Let us drink wine and bless each other's futures. I will always remain in your debt and be your faithful friend.'

She smiled and sat down on a velvet cushion that had been placed on the floor, the embroidered cover shining in the firelight. Her gown spread out around her like a rippling silver pool. Will reached down to touch the silky fabric and traced his fingers up to the ribbon ties at her throat. She shivered at the gentle touch, and he drew back quickly.

'I find it hard not to touch you,' he whispered. 'But do not fear — I am not a man who breaks his word.'

Pouring two glasses of wine, he gave her one and sat beside her. She looked around the room, seeing the care he had taken to make it special for her. It seemed such a shame he would never have a true wife to look after and love. She glanced at him again, their gaze holding over the glass of crimson wine he had raised to his mouth.

'What are you thinking about?' he said.

Elizabeth took a deep breath. 'Joan said you had been wed before.'

8

The glass shook in Will's hand and he lowered it to the floor. His mother had been right — he should have told Elizabeth earlier.

'I'm sorry for not telling you, but it was hard to find the words.'

Elizabeth looked at him, her dark blue eyes gazing into his and the scent of her perfume oil filling the air.

'Tell me about her,' she said.

'Her name was Adela and she was sixteen, a year younger than I. Her family were wealthy, and my father pushed for the match as he was in debt and fearful of prison.'

'Did you want to marry her?'

He looked at her, seeing a flicker of hurt in her beautiful eyes. Had she started to care for him in the way he feared he did for her?

'My father would have sent me from

Shorecross if I'd refused. Joan was only thirteen and I feared for her safety. I knew Adela to be a kind girl, who I could be happy with.'

'Did you love her?'

Had he loved Adela? Her face appeared in his mind and he closed his eyes. Putting his glass on the table, he rose and went over to the window where, opening the shutter, he rested his elbows on the sill and breathed in the cool, crisp air.

'I'm sorry, I shouldn't have asked,' Elizabeth said. 'It clearly pains you still.'

He pictured Adela's smooth light brown hair and clear green eyes, thought of her smile and the warm touch of her shy, hesitant body.

'I cared for her, but I don't know if it was love. I was very young.'

Elizabeth parted her lips, but instead of speaking, she touched her mouth with her fingertips as if reminding herself to remain silent and let him speak.

'Adela became pregnant very quickly,'

he said. 'Within two months of the wedding.'

'So you are a father?' she said.

Will closed his eyes. 'I was never a father; my child never breathed. The birth was horrific and neither survived.'

Her hand, warm and firm, slid into his and squeezed tight.

'I took Adela back to her father for burial. When he saw her coffin, he tried to attack me with an axe, tears streaming down his cheeks.'

'But it was not your fault. It is a very common for woman to die in childbirth.'

'Common? Yes, I know it is common. My mother lost two babies because they grew too big for safe birthing. She only just survived, and after Joan, she bore no more. It's a family trait. My son grew the same way, and Adela was a tiny girl. She died after three days of dreadful suffering.' He closed his eyes. 'I remember her screams still.'

Her hands tightened.

'It must have been terrible, I cannot

imagine your pain,' she said. 'But that still doesn't make it your fault. Childbirth is part of life and living. Where would we be if no more children were born?'

'They won't be born due to me. I vowed then that I would never again be responsible for the death of a woman.'

Elizabeth moistened her lips. 'Have there been no other women since?'

He shook his head.

Elizabeth slid her arms around him, resting against his back and holding him tight. He turned and relaxed against her, desperate for the comfort of her warm body. Breathing in the scent of her lavender perfume, he pushed his hands into her hair, the strands heavy and alive in his hands. He trailed his fingers down her cheek, gaze fastened on hers, then his hands smoothed over her neck and shoulders.

'We should sleep,' he said, his voice hoarse.

★ ★ ★

Will lay on the rug, covered in a blanket, as the early-morning rain patted against the windows. A thin strip of grey showed through the centre of the closed shutters. He should have been in the fields by now, but instead of getting up, he looked at the sleeping girl on the bed. Elizabeth's thick dark hair spread in tangles over the pillow, and the bed covers' position revealed her ivory shoulders.

The light from the ill-fitting shutters lightened to a pale cream and he frowned, wishing the sun would slow its steady rise. It seemed cruel to desert Elizabeth the day after their wedding. Why couldn't the border lords fight their own battles? Why should he be involved? At first, he had hoped the summons was a mistake, but the Earl of Northumberland had confirmed in a terse letter that it was genuine. It had been a long time since he rode in battle.

The heavy clop of oxen hooves came from outside, and he slowly sat up. This was his last day at Shorecross and he had to ensure everything was done. Elizabeth and the steward would be in charge during his absence. She seemed confident, but he was still worried. Did she know enough? Her uncle's farm was much smaller.

Putting his bare foot on the floor, a hard, cold shape pressed under his instep and he pulled his leg back up. It was only a glass, though, which they must have dropped without noticing the previous night. He smiled and put it back on the table.

Goosebumps rose on his skin in the cold air. Alice had not been in to light the fire. Either she was recovering from the festivities, or too afraid of finding her master and mistress sprawled together in wanton love.

Walking to his dressing room, he snatched a shirt from the back of a chair in his dressing room and pulled it over his head. Swiftly, he pulled on his hose and breeches. In truth, it probably was a good time to go to Scotland; he needed space from Elizabeth. She was proving more dangerous to his peace of mind than Edmund. Returning to the bedroom, Will knelt by the empty fireplace and arranged sticks from the basket. Flicking a flint and steel, he held them to a piece of old cloth from the basket and watched the fabric glow crimson before dropping it by the twigs. The wood crackled and he breathed in the scent of woodsmoke.

Disturbed by the noise, Elizabeth moved on the bed, pulling the covers higher and snuggling against the pillow. Her eyes were closed in sleep, eyelashes forming little dark arches on her cheeks, her hair loose on the bedsheets in the way only a husband should see.

Rising, he strode back into his dressing room and picked up his high riding boots, sitting on a stool to pull them up. Then he dropped his head into his hands. He had to get control of himself, remind himself of his duty to protect Shorecross. He and Elizabeth could never be anything more than friends.

From the bedroom came the sound of bare feet on floorboards; glancing up, he saw her standing in the doorway.

'You make it very difficult to go,' he said, gazing at her.

'Stay, then.'

'I must work.' He reached for her hand and held it, warm, in his own.

'I fear for you in Scotland.' Her voice was low.

'There's nothing to be afraid of. I've survived many battles. Those with titles are usually ransomed rather then killed, so you might get a large bill for me in a month's time.' He kissed her hand and let it go. 'It is up to you to decide if I am worth paying for.'

'It depends on the price. I am in need of new gowns.'

'You would replace me with a dress?'

'Well, if it is a gown made from cloth of gold . . . '

He laughed and she smiled.

'No, my lord, I would not let them keep you.' She took a step back, then looked at him, her blue eyes anxious.

'How could we pay your ransom? Can we sell Shorecross if need be?'

He shook his head. 'It is entailed to the next heir; even I cannot sell Shorecross.' She tensed and he lightened his tone. 'The Scots would not want me anyway — a mere lord of the manor — and we have our English archers to defend us.' He rose to his feet. 'Let's not spend our last day talking of war. Fetch your clothes. We'll sneak out for a ride in the sunrise while our guests slumber. I need to explain the workings of the estate to you, since it is too large for Mother and the steward to manage alone.'

* * *

Elizabeth trotted her horse into the courtyard, the clop of hooves of Will's horse echoing behind her. Her stomach rumbled as she breathed in the scent of fresh bread and roasting pork from the outdoor kitchen. She'd eaten a slice of bread and beef before her ride, but they'd been out most of the morning. Will had shown her the small tenanted farms he owned and the livestock on the common land. It was information she needed to know, but if she was honest, she'd have preferred to spend their last day talking about things other than sheep. But Will he took his responsibilities to the estate seriously, and after hearing about his father, it was of no wonder.

Glancing back at him over her shoulder, her chest tightened — she didn't want him to leave today. The weather reflected her mood with its hard daggers of rain that lashed her hood. The hooves of her horse splashed through puddles in the yard, soaking her legs. The animal would need a good rub-down today. Reaching the stable, she pulled on the reins, then her mouth dropped open.

Tied outside the stable, loaded with bags, were two familiar mounts and a donkey. Surely Uncle Walter wouldn't travel home in this weather? She had hoped that he would stay longer, as his presence had been a comfort. Her uncle stepped out of the manor house and reached up to take the bridle of her horse.

'I've been looking for you.'

Elizabeth slid down. 'Are you leaving?'

'I have to, but I'll return in the summer.'

'Please stay a little longer, I'll miss you.'

'I must go, my dear. Your aunt can't manage the farm alone for long.' He embraced her. 'Take care, and send a messenger if you need me. If the roads remain clear, perhaps you and Lord Downes could visit us? I would be delighted to show him around.'

Elizabeth swallowed. How lovely it would be to visit her childhood home with Will, but their marriage would be over by then. She wiped her eyes.

'Thank you for coming, Uncle. It meant a lot to me.'

'I promised your father I would take

care of you.' He squeezed her arm. 'Lord Downes seems a good man, but if you are unhappy, come straight home. You'll always be welcome.'

'Thank you. I am settled here though.'

'I am glad to hear it.'

The sound of hooves splashing through the puddles came from behind as Will drew his horse in, before swinging from the saddle.

'I'm sorry you have to leave us, Walter. Take care on the journey home.'

Walter climbed onto his horse. 'Thank you, sir, and good bye.' He flicked his reins.

Elizabeth watched him trot out the gate, tears in her eyes. As kind as the Downes family had been, her future at Shorecross was uncertain. Pulling her hood close to her head, she looked at her soaked horse when the creature shivered under the strong wind.

'Let's get you dry,' she said, leading the mare to the stable.

A boy standing in the doorway

reached out and took the reins.

'She'll need a good rub-down, please,' Elizabeth said.

'Yes, my lady.' He bowed.

She turned towards the house, when loud, rancorous voices floated over the wall from the lane leading to the estate. Glancing at the gate, she drew a sharp breath. It had been left unguarded, the men likely taking shelter from the rain. The noise increased, mingled now with marching feet and the jingle of metal.

'Will?' she said. 'Will? Is it Edmund?'

Sword already drawn, Will moved towards the gate, treading the cautious step of an experienced soldier.

Armed men flooded in through the entrance and Elizabeth jumped back, glancing at the house. But the young boy stood still beside her, holding her horse, as he gazed at the newcomers in fascination. She could not flee when a child stood so brave! And what of Joan and Margaret in the house? Her place was here, no matter what trouble these invaders brought.

'What do they want?' she called.

Will strode over to the men. 'You're early.'

Elizabeth frowned. Who were they? None of them wore livery, clad instead in an assortment of helmets and jerkins. But each was armed with a sword and a mace.

'Will?'

He glanced back. 'It's the mercenaries I hired for Scotland. They were to arrive here this evening for us to travel to the border together.'

Elizabeth looked at the soldiers.

'Do they need feeding? Should I organise bread and ale?'

'No, they arrange their own food. I pay them extra.'

'Then I had better warn Joan and Margaret about their presence. Joan doesn't need any shocks at the moment.'

★   ★   ★

Will waved the last of his wedding guests out of the gate. His friends had all made a sudden exit upon spotting the soldiers, and he couldn't blame them.

The mercenaries had spread out across the yard, padded gambeson jackets stained and — he suspected — reeking of sweat. A pile of axes and maces lay on the floor, mixed up with cloaks and blankets, all thrown carelessly down. Two men with long beards and greasy hair rested against the wall of the well, talking to Alice as she drew up the bucket. The girl was startled and grabbed the bucket so fast she tipped it over the ground.

Will went over to help, but Elizabeth had stepped out of the house.

'Don't worry, Alice. Go back to the Great Hall,' she said, then crossed the yard towards him. 'I warned your mother and sister. But they are coming out anyway to say goodbye. Do you have to go straight away?'

'I can't leave this lot milling around the yard.' He kicked a pack out of his way. 'Robert! Saddle my charger.'

'All done, master, and your body servant is bringing your armour. I assume you won't ride in it?'

'Not yet; we've a long march before we even reach the borders.'

He looked at the mercenaries. It would have been a much quicker trip had they been mounted, but supplying horses for a hundred men was beyond his pocket.

Elizabeth gave a sharp intake of breath and he turned to see what had disturbed her.

His servants were stumbling across the mud, carrying his armour. The silver metal gleamed under the weak light, glossy with rain, and the leather straps hung loose to the ground. Robert carried a helmet, visor shut tight, showing dark and vacant eye-slits. In his other hand, he swung a mace by the shaft, the hard metal club end striking the floor with a sharp thud.

Elizabeth raised a hand to her mouth.

'Don't look so shocked, girl,' Margaret said, stepping out the house with Joan beside her. 'It's designed to protect him.'

'I am sorry,' Elizabeth said. 'It unnerved me. He is truly going to war. I hadn't understood before.' Her face paled, and Will put his arm about her shoulder.

'William, I want you to take Robert with you,' Margaret said.

'No,' he said.

'If you're killed without a male heir, we are all homeless.'

He winced; she knew where to hit him.

'Take Robert, please,' Elizabeth said. 'We have the rest of your garrison here.'

Will looked at the hired soldiers; they would be hard to manage alone.

'All right. Robert, gather what you need. We're leaving immediately.'

'Yes sir,' Robert said, and grinned.

Will held Elizabeth's hand, his chest constricting at the sight of her tears.

Had it only been yesterday that they wed? She slid her arms around his neck, and he breathed deeply, fixing the scent of her perfume oil in his mind.

'Be careful,' she said.

'Of course. And keep a lookout for Edmund. I'll be back as soon as I can.' He glanced at the mercenaries with tight lips as one urinated outside the kitchen block. 'And I will happily leave this lot behind in Scotland.'

★ ★ ★

Elizabeth stood by the entrance to the narrow lane until Will had vanished from sight. Tears pricked her eyes and she wiped them away with an impatient hand.

'Come on, Elizabeth. No moping. We have work to do. Shorecross doesn't run itself,' Margaret said.

Elizabeth nodded slowly, turning to look at the fields which stretched into the distance. Now the master had gone, she was in charge. Such a huge responsibility! Well, she would have to learn fast. Will had trusted her to care for his estate and family, and she could not let him down.

9

Strong winds billowed out the long line of campaign tents, and Will's horse jerked beneath him as the frayed fabric flared in front of them. He tightened his grip on the reins. Although he rode a battle-trained destrier, it had been several years since they had both been to war.

Will glanced back to check Robert and the mercenaries were close behind, then jumped as a huge boom shook the ground. From the training ground, a red flash flared, followed by a heavy thud and the acrid smell of gunpowder. Pulling a scarf up to his nose and mouth, he coughed when the foul stink of open latrines and sweat replaced that of the explosives — the odour hanging so thickly in the air that he tasted the sharp salty rank in his throat. Attracted by the nearby marshes, a cloud of mosquitoes hovered around his face, and he waved his hand to dispel them.

'Downes! Hey, Downes!'

A man dressed in the full armour of a knight stood beside the path ahead. It was impossible to see the man's face under his visor, but his voice was unmistakable. It was Hugh Conrad, his old battle companion.

Will grinned and reined in his horse.

'Hugh,' he said. 'How are things?'

'Better now you're here.' Hugh removed his helmet. 'I wasn't expecting you to join us on the field.'

'It's not through choice.'

'I doubt many of us would choose this. How's that pretty sister of yours?'

'Fine.' Will looked away briefly.

'Excellent.' Hugh eyed the mercenaries. 'I've lost a good few to camp sickness, if you want to join me. Are they infantry?'

'Axe and mace; a few are trained to the pike, and three can use cannon. They're all experienced.'

'Wonderful. Leave them with me

while you report to Northumberland's son. Do they need feeding?'

'If you've got enough supplies. It's been a long trip and they've marched far.'

'I'll ask the women to make pottage.' He glanced at Will's doublet. 'You'll need to put your armour on before you see Henry Percy; he likes to see commandeers battle-ready.'

'I'm not here to command.' His brow creased. 'To be honest, I'm not quite sure why I *am* here.'

Hugh pressed his lips together. 'It's pretty bad. Parts of Northumberland and Cumbria have been burned to the ground.'

'I saw.'

Will's hands tightened to his reins as he remembered the black-beamed burnt houses and patches of thick, sticky, dried blood in the villages they had passed. A couple of villagers had stopped him, their eyes red with weeping and mouths set in a hard splinter of hatred as they begged to join him. Throat constricted, he had refused. Battles needed steady minds, and one desperate father could put all his men in danger.

Will shook his head to dispel the image.

'Robert,' he said, 'you go with the men, whilst I pay a visit to Lord Henry Percy.'

Robert slid down from his mount and glanced behind him.

'Come on men,' he said to the mercenaries. 'Let's find hot stew and cold ale.'

Relieved to have a few minutes alone, Will trotted down the mud path, his heartbeat speeding at the familiar sounds of battle preparation. Hidden somewhere in the hills around them was the Scots army, led by the Earl of Douglas. He glanced briefly at the surrounding land, but wasn't too concerned. The English army lost few of their battles, and, looking at the hundreds of pitched tents and wagons filled with arrows, he was certain they would not lose this one.

It had been good fortune to meet Hugh. The man was an experienced warrior, whilst his own skills had rusted. A large white pavilion ahead glowed pink under the red sunset; turning the horse, he headed towards it. A group of armed men stood outside, stepping forward quickly as he swung down from his saddle. Immediately, his boot sank into thick mud and he yanked it free, grimacing at the foul stench. The place was a filthy mire compared to the clean, fresh fields of Shorecross.

He wouldn't leave his horse alone here, either: they were often stolen. Instead he led it to a young boy.

'Take care of my mount, and there's a silver coin when I return.'

Stepping back to the tent, he bowed at the knights outside.

'Lord William Downes, Baron of Shorecross. I've brought the men requested by Lord Northumberland. Is he available?'

'No, but his son is.'

'I'll see him, then.'

The man jerked his finger at the tent and Will stepped in, a creak of armour coming from behind as two of the knights followed. He smiled — in his hose and a jerkin, he could easily outrun them.

'Hand me your sword,' a man said.

Will's hand shot to his belt. Since the attack by Edmund, he had never been without it, but the guards wouldn't allow him to go any further armed. Unbuckling the weapon, he held it out slowly.

'Thank you, sir.' A knight grabbed it and thrust it into the ground outside.

'Come with me,' another man said.

Will walked behind him, his lip curling up as he stared at the heavy oak furniture and thick silk hangings inside the tent. Without such comforts, the army could have travelled several miles a day faster. When on campaign, he'd always slept in a basic tent and taken meals at a communal fire.

169

The knight led him to a brazier that spat out heat and the scent of burning wood. Will turned as footsteps sounded behind; a man in his late twenties strode towards him. Clad in mail, hand on his sword, the man raised his eyebrows enquiringly.

Will bowed. The man's air of authority meant he could only be Henry Percy, son of the Earl of Northumberland.

'Lord Downes,' Henry Percy said. 'You're later than expected. And where is your armour?'

Will stopped himself from remarking that he would have been even later if he had ridden fully-armoured.

'I have brought one hundred mercenaries,' he said.

'Good. They're needed as the Scots are destroying our villages. I was told you were eager to join us. Do you have land up here?'

Will shook his head slowly. 'Who told you I was eager, my lord?'

'Your friend — Edwin, or something

like that. I can't remember. You've seen action before, I believe?'

'Do you mean Edmund?' Will's mouth went dry. 'Is he still here?'

'I believe he has left. Were you anxious to see him?'

'He is no friend of mine.'

'Oh, well, I understand enemies.' Henry smiled. 'But yours is now Douglas, Earl of Ormand. Your petty quarrel with Edwin can wait.'

Will curled his fists. The nerve of the man! But of course, Henry Percy didn't understand the significance of the situation.

'My Lord, I must go. My family are in danger from Edmund; he holds a grudge against us and my womenfolk are alone.' Will turned around, looking for his sword.

'I hope you aren't thinking of leaving us?' Henry Percy said.

Will twisted back and gave a sharp bow. 'I'm sorry, my lord, but I must. I will leave my men here under the charge of Hugh Conrad.'

'You're going nowhere.'

'That man intends to kill my family. Do you not understand that?'

Henry's fingers tapped his sword. 'I understand the concern for your family, but I'm certain a man of your background would have left his home well-guarded. They'll be fine, and I have need of your services.'

'I cannot stay.'

Henry's face darkened. 'Desert, and I'll have you executed — a traitor's death. Do you understand?'

Will bowed.

'Good. You may withdraw,' Henry Percy said.

Will strode back outside, yanking his sword from the ground and sheathing it. What a fool he had been! Despite Henry Percy's threat, he had to get back to Shorecross. Snatching his reins from the waiting boy, he tossed the lad a coin, and galloped down the path.

'My lord!'

Will pulled hard on the reins. Robert stood by the side of the road, waving.

'Get the packs, we have to go,' Will said. 'Edmund's on his way to Shore-cross.'

Robert cursed. 'I'll get my horse.' He ran off.

Will tapped his reins impatiently, checking behind to make sure he was not being pursued. The path was clear, except for two women carrying water jugs.

'Ready, sir,' Robert said, leading two horses up the path, one loaded with packs. Hugh walked beside him, frowning.

'What took so long?' Will demanded of Robert.

'Sir, I was minutes.'

'What's going on, William?' Hugh said.

'Can I leave my men with you?'

'I'm happy to have them, but why are you going?'

'My family are in danger. I've been tricked into leaving Shorecross.'

'Shall I come too?'

Will remembered Henry Percy's

threat of execution.

'No, stay here, I'll be in touch. Get mounted, Robert, we must go!'

★　★　★

Elizabeth closed the ledger with a bang and drummed her fingers on the brown leather cover. It had surprised her to discover how large the Shorecross estate was. No wonder Will often looked so exhausted. She had assumed the surrounding lands were the sum of the estate, but there were also farms held by tenants, several mills, and numerous bakehouses. The farms at Shorecross were profitable, but the mills and bakehouses were not, since it appeared his workers never paid to have their wheat ground or bread cooked.

Knowing Will as she did, she didn't press for the monies. It was almost certainly deliberate, with the costs covered by yields from the other businesses.

Remembering Will, she opened a

drawer and took out a silk parcel. It had haunted her since she had discovered it the previous night. Folding back the delicate fabric, she stared at a tiny pair of woollen bootees. Yellow with age, they had been knitted with care, and tied with a white ribbon. Beside them lay a sprig of a dried rose, but whether it was from Adela's wedding bouquet or funeral wreath, she didn't know.

The shoes were so small.

She swallowed a lump in her throat. It was no wonder he wasn't ready to wed again — it was likely he never would be. Someone knocked on the door, and she quickly wrapped the precious items up and returned them to the drawer.

'Yes?' she said.

Margaret opened the door. 'Are you busy?'

'Come in. Was the midwife any good?' Elizabeth turned to put the ledgers back on the shelf.

'I think so. She's experienced, and has a birthing chair: all the fashion in

Germany, apparently.'

'Will it help?'

'I'm not sure.' Margaret sat down on the spare chair. 'She says Joan is very big for seven months.'

Elizabeth nodded, having privately thought the same thing.

'Will told me about Adela,' she said. 'I'm sorry.'

Margaret looked down, her eyes distant. 'She was a tiny girl and suffered badly. We didn't realise when Will married her — that large babies were a curse in our family.'

Elizabeth reached out to squeeze her mother-in-law's hand. 'I understand you had problems too?'

Margaret hesitated. 'William was my firstborn and he survived, but I lost the next two. They were both large babies and got stuck, the same as happened to Adela. The physician told me not to have any more, but my husband did not pay heed, and I fell pregnant again.' Margaret stopped. 'Will was still very young, and would have suffered under

176

the drunken care of his father.'

'I understand,' Elizabeth said, her voice gentle.

'I tried to bring on an early labour. Judge me if you will, but I had no choice. Joan was born before she ought to have been, but we both survived. And after her, there were no more babies, and I thought that was the end of it. I never expected Adela to have the same problem.'

Elizabeth briefly closed her eyes. 'I'm sorry for your losses; it must have been a terrible time.'

'You're a good girl,' Margaret said, her voice gruff. 'And if Joan can be delivered safely of a living child, you will have your heir. Then you won't have to suffer the way Adela had to, and my son won't lose a second wife.'

Elizabeth looked up, startled, and her stomach churned.

'William was only seventeen when he lost his wife and son. I didn't think he would ever recover,' Margaret said. 'Then he brought you home, and I can see how happy he is. He loves you. Whatever agreements you have made about your marriage are between the two of you.'

Elizabeth remembered the tiny boo-tees. How this family had suffered!

Then the door was pushed open and Alice put her head around, holding a letter. 'For Lady Joan.'

'I'll see she gets it,' Elizabeth said, reaching up to take the sealed note. In curiosity, she glanced at the name and a cold shiver ran up her back. It was the same sloping scrawl that had signed her bridal contract. Edmund's.

Her fingers loosened on the letter and it fell to the desk. What was she to do? She could not open her sister-in-law's message, but neither did she want to give her a letter from Edmund. Her fingers pressed hard on the paper as she tried to make out the words inside. But it was thick parchment and impreg-nable. Maybe if she held it to the light? She picked it up and turned towards the window, then stopped. Even if it was from Edmund, it had been addressed to her sister-in-law.

'What is the matter?' Margaret said.

'I believe this note is from Edmund.'

Margaret grabbed the letter, broke the seal and opened it.

'We must contact Will,' she said. 'Edmund has asked Joan to meet him on the evening of the twenty-first of October.'

'She must not.' Elizabeth rose to her feet. Turning, she looked through the window. Where was Edmund? Raising a hand to her face, she remembered his blows.

'He's her husband. Maybe he intends to return to her?' Margaret said.

'He intends to kill her.'

Margaret jumped.

'Believe me,' Elizabeth said. 'I know him, he seeks revenge on Will.'

'On William?'

Elizabeth drew a sharp breath, picturing Will and Robert riding to Scotland. He had been right to be suspicious. Had Edmund lain in wait for him? No, he *must* be alive; surely she would sense if he was not?

'Elizabeth?'

She looked at the frightened eyes of his mother.

'I'm sure he is fine,' she said. 'He is a gifted swordsman.'

Margaret turned to leave, then stopped and looked back.

'How do you know Edmund?'

Elizabeth closed her eyes. How could she explain that she'd been betrothed to this woman's son-in-law?

10

'Two days ago, you say?' Will said, resting his hand on his sword.

The innkeeper looked uneasy.

'Yes, fitting that description. He had a group of men with him — ruffians. That's why I remembered him, as my wife wasn't happy about them staying.'

'Thanks.'

Dropping a coin onto a trestle table, Will pushed his way back through the crowded room and out the door. On the grass verge outside, Robert waited with the horses, his face pale and thick black shadows under his eyes.

'Any news?' Robert said.

'Edmund passed by two days ago.' Will swung himself into his saddle. 'Can you ride all night? If not, I'll have to go on alone, since we're so close to Shorecross.'

Robert gave him a look of contempt.

With a brief, tight smile, Will flicked the reins as the tired animal shuddered. 'Good boy, I'll take it out of his flesh for you,' he whispered, patting the horse's shoulder.

*   *   *

'Why are you carrying a carving knife?' Joan said.

Elizabeth stopped outside her chamber door and glanced down at the gleaming metal blade that had cut through the scarf she'd wrapped around it. She must have overdone the sharpening.

'I fancied a late-night apple.'

Joan snorted. 'So nothing to do with the extra men guarding the gate? Will's only been gone a few weeks, and you've turned the place into the Tower of London.' She reached out and touched Elizabeth's arm. 'I know it can seem daunting to manage Shorecross without him, but honestly, we'll survive. He often goes away on business.'

Heat flooded Elizabeth's cheeks, and she stopped herself from protesting that she was quite capable of taking care of the estate. It was impossible to know how much loyalty the other girl still had to Edmund, and Elizabeth hadn't really known her long enough to understand her character. What if she was not as innocent as she appeared? She looked at her sister-in-law's wide smile. Surely Joan could not be double-crossing them? But she had been dishonest before by marrying in secret.

A thud came from outside the window, and she jumped.

'It's a branch falling,' Joan said.

'Yes, of course it is. Now, I must get to bed. Are you all right? Do you need anything?'

'I'm going to walk up and down the corridor since my back's aching. So please don't attack me if you hear footsteps.'

Elizabeth closed her chamber door and dropped onto the bed. Joan would think her insane soon. Actually, she did feel like she was going mad. It was the intolerable waiting for Edmund to arrive. How strong was his wish for vengeance? Strong enough for murder?

Raising the edge of her mattress, she shoved the knife between the sheet and headboard before climbing under the covers and lying still, hugging her knees. On a nearby chest, a candle flickered under the draught from the shutters. Hopefully it would not blow out. From the corridor came the light pacing of Joan, the sound alarming rather than comforting her. From outside in the courtyard, a guard shouted, 'Change watch!'

Elizabeth's shoulders relaxed. Of course there was nothing to worry about, not when the men of Shorecross were watching the gate, weapons drawn. It was just the waiting that played on her nerves. She yawned, rubbing her sore eyes. It had been two days since she slept properly, and it would be impossible to stay up another night. It was time to trust the soldiers to defend their master's land.

She dozed against the pillows, as the soft shuffle of Joan pacing drifted from the hall.

★   ★   ★

Elizabeth opened her eyes, muscles tense. What had woken her? Her candle still glowed on the chest with a tiny pinprick of yellow flame, and no sound came from the corridor. Joan must have finally gone to bed. She snuggled back under the covers and sleepily turned over. Then a hand gripped her shoulder.

She froze. Who sat on the bed beside her?

The hand tightened — fingers snapping around her flesh like a wolf grabbing its prey. Elizabeth screamed, but a palm slammed over her mouth and sharp knees pressed against her hips, as a heavy weight jumped onto her, pinning her to the mattress. Foul breath, reeking of ale and rotting meat, filled her nose. In horror, she recognized the stench. Edmund.

A groan came from the floor; twisting her head to look, her eyes opened wide. A long white shape, the length of a person, lay on her bedroom floor. Who was it? Had Edmund caught Will?

'Keep still,' Edmund hissed.

Elizabeth drew a desperate breath as his hand pressed tighter against her mouth and she tasted the sweat on his unwashed skin. Her stomach churned; gagging, she struggled again, but he thrust his knee into her abdomen and she gasped.

'Promise not to scream?' he said.

Elizabeth nodded, warm tears spilling down her cheeks. Turning her head, she peered at the floor again. Joan lay crumpled on the floorboards, with her white nightgown pulled up to her thighs and a heavy black gag tied around her mouth. Eyes, wide and scared, stared at Elizabeth.

'Let me help her. What did you do?' Elizabeth said.

'Not what I had planned.' His teeth flashed in the candlelight. 'I wasn't expecting the massive belly on her. Repulsive. I assume it's mine?'

Elizabeth moistened her lips. If he knew the child was his, would he be more likely to let Joan go? Or to kill her?

'Yes. It's yours, and heir to Shorecross.'

'I reckon Lord Downes would rather torch the place then let my child inherit.'

'You're wrong!' The knife pressed against her throat again and she lowered her voice. 'Will has arranged for the child to inherit Shorecross, so let Joan go.'

Joan's eyes stared frantically over the long strip of black material around her mouth, and she drummed her tied heels on the floor.

Nausea rose from Elizabeth's stomach and she stared at a tic jerking in the corner of Edmund's eye, twisting his features. A thin, new scar with plucked red skin wove across his jaw, mingling with his dark, stubbly beard; and a long, dark, old fashioned robe hung from his shoulders.

'Where is Will?' she said.

'He'll be too late.'

Her shoulder slumped in relief. At least her husband was alive. She glanced at the fist holding the knife to her throat: on the back of his hand, the skin was purple and swollen.

'You didn't want Will to be here?' she said, keeping the conversation going, as she looked back at the gangrenous wound. A trickle of cloudy pus oozed out.

'He'll come home to find his house burnt to the ground and family charred in the ruins. He'll know it was me, but will never be able to prove it.'

'He'll hunt you down.'

'It won't do any good. I've passage booked on a boat to France tonight.'

She looked towards the window. Would a single scream alert the guards? But he must have guessed her thoughts, because the blade tightened.

'I wouldn't bother, I didn't come alone. Your men are dead, or dying, along with your maid.'

'Alice? Does she live?' She drew in a sharp breath.

'Not anymore.'

Hot, angry tears filled her eyes, then the candle flickered again and she glanced towards it.

'May I see if my sister-in-law is all right?' she said.

Edmund grasped her hair and, with the blade pressed against the skin beneath her ear, allowed her to look down her side of the bed. Joan's chest lifted in sharp, shallow breaths; the gag was clearly so thick and tight around her mouth, she was having problems taking in enough air.

'Let me loosen it,' Elizabeth said. 'You don't want her to die just yet, surely? Not when you made such good plans to burn us.'

The knife pressed against her skin and she bit back a scream. Who else had he killed? Were she and Joan alone in Shorecross, surrounded by corpses?

'Lie down on the bed,' Edmund said, his mouth close to her ear.

Elizabeth swallowed. 'I want to push her gag down, so she can breathe. Then I'll let you do as you wish.' She glanced at the candle again.

His hand gripped her shoulder, but she refused to look at him.

'You can do it that way,' she said. 'But since I'll fight you, it'll be harder.'

'Scream, or try to run, and I'll kill her,' he said.

Edmund shoved her feet off the bed and Elizabeth lowered herself down to the floorboards, his knife pressing against the back of her neck. He sat on the edge of the bed with his robes dangling to the floor, and she calmly picked up the candle from the chest as if it had been part of their agreement.

Elizabeth leaned forward to ease the gag away from Joan's nose as the girl struggled against her bonds.

'I think you might have a lump on

your head,' she said. 'Let me see. Move your head a little — oh, what was that noise?' she added suddenly in a whisper.

Edmund laughed. 'Do you think I'm that stupid?' But he glanced towards the door.

Elizabeth thrust her lit candle against the trailing ends of his robe and, when the loose threads glowed red, whipped the candle back and put it on the chest. A burning smell drifted across the room and Edmund sniffed.

The tiny glow crept up the trailing edges of his robe. Elizabeth watched it from the corner of her eye. He hadn't noticed.

'Why are you doing this?' she said.

'You cheated me. You deserve it.'

'How did I cheat you?'

'You didn't give your lands, the ones you promised I could have.'

'But they aren't worth anything!'

He smiled. 'Back on the bed.'

Trembling, Elizabeth lay down, putting a hand up as if to support her head. Her fingers pushed down against the headboard, reaching for the knife, as wisps of grey smoke drifted from the floor.

'Hey!' Edmund cried, then grabbed his robe, stamped on the hem.

Elizabeth screamed, the sound echoing around the room, leaving her throat burning.

'You witch!' he said, grabbing the candle and Elizabeth's arm.

She struggled, but he brought the flame against her skin and she yelled again as a searing pain flared over her flesh. Then, jerking sideways, she flung her arm out, the knife in her hand.

It drove into his shoulder and he leapt back, dropping the candle onto the floor. The room dimmed. He grasped her legs and she kicked out violently, then the chamber door was flung back. A figure stood in the doorway, clad in a long white nightgown and clutching a lamp.

'Let her go!' Margaret ordered.

'Move, and I'll run her through,' Edmund said.

'What do you want? Money? I can get money.'

'And of course you won't rouse a dozen servants as well.'

'What have you done to my daughter?'

'I'm saving her for later.'

Joan moaned, and Elizabeth looked down at where she lay on the floor. It would destroy Will if he returned to find his family slaughtered. How dare Edmund threaten this household twice! She remembered the humiliations she had suffered at his hands on the road — the starving, the slaps — and her fists tightened. What a dreadful life he'd planned for her. This hideous, foul man who believed he had all the power, when in fact he was worth nothing.

Twisting her body to the side, she kicked out viciously, her heel cracking hard down on Edmund's knee. He snarled and threw himself on her, but with muscles honed by horse-riding,

Elizabeth struck out with her feet again, catching him on the chest in a solid thump that echoed around the room.

'Margaret, grab him!'

Her mother-in-law leapt forward and threw her arms around him, pinning him back as he struggled. In a move she must have learnt from her violent husband, she slammed the palm of her hand against his nose, and he howled.

Flinging herself on the bed, Elizabeth felt for her knife and yanked it out. Could she do it? Could she stab another person? If she did not, they were all dead. Inhaling sharply, she lashed out in the darkness, and there was a sickening thud as the blade sank into flesh. Then he grabbed her and she screamed.

'Give me that knife!' he yelled, wrestling it from her grip.

She twisted the blade again, cutting into his sleeve and he yelped, pulling back.

'Get out! Now, before I stab you again!' Elizabeth shouted.

He took a step back, then tensed, prepared to jump again. But he was weakening: blood poured from his hand, spreading in a pool on the floor. She must have hit a vein.

From the corner of the room came a slight click. Elizabeth looked towards the dressing-room door at the gap that had appeared down the side of the frame. It widened, sending a spike of moonlight across the dark floor-boards.

Then Will and Robert leapt into the room, swords drawn.

'Get down!' Will shouted.

Elizabeth flung herself onto the mattress and jumped at the clash of swords. Turning her head, she cried out as Will drew back his sword and ran Edmund through. For a moment, the man stood still, then his legs folded beneath him and he collapsed to the floor, face white and eyes unseeing. She stared at his corpse, then her head whirled and a nauseating dizziness took her into blackness.

Someone stroked her hair and, moaning, she tried to turn over.

'Keep still,' Will said.

She opened her eyes.

'The physician said not to let you move.'

'Is everyone else all right? Alice?'

'Your maid has a lump the size of a duck egg on her head, but she'll be fine, and Mother is sitting with her. Alice is a brave girl.'

'I feared she was dead.'

'So did I when I saw her. We lost three men at the gate, though.'

A streak of anger flared through her exhausted body. How dare Edmund kill Shorecross men?

'There was nothing you could have done,' he said.

Elizabeth shivered. Best not to think about it; Edmund had been planning a worse fate for her and Joan.

Instead, she looked around the unfamiliar chamber.

'Where am I?'

'It's the room my father slept in. Mother redecorated it after he died, but neither of us fancied sleeping here. Since your room has Edmund's corpse on the floor, and mine . . . ' He hesitated. ' . . . has the ghost of Adela, I decided it was time for us to use this one.'

'Was my old room hers?'

'Yes.'

Elizabeth nodded; she had suspected as much. The second door into the dressing-room had been built for a reason: it was a suite intended for a husband and wife. Had Adela and Will slept in one bed through the night, or had she slipped back to her own room? She shook her head. It wasn't healthy to think of such things. The girl had died.

She looked at the large expanse of bed beside her. Did Will intend to sleep beside her? Picturing him lying there, eyes closed and hair loose on the pillow, a cold chill went down her spine. What would become of them both now? Since Edmund was dead, there was no longer any need for them to stay together. A legitimate son of Joan's could inherit the estate. Will loved her, she suspected, but a man of his principles would stick by his decision to never take a true wife. Soon she would have to leave Shorecross, and him.

'Are you staying here too?' she asked.

'I fear to let you out of my sight at the moment.' He squeezed her hand. 'It is your decision, but we can lie in bed together, if you would let me.'

It would be better if he did not, since it could only make the final split more painful. She opened her mouth to tell him, but looked into his chestnut eyes and said nothing. She could not bear the thought of being parted from him.

Will rose. 'I'm going to arrange you some food; then, after checking on Joan, I'll bring the estate books up and work beside you.' He went to the door, then looked back. 'There is nothing to be afraid of now.'

She smiled, but in truth, she would now will Edmund back into life if the alternative was to lose her husband.

11

'Elizabeth!' Will shouted.

Wearing her bright red habit and mounted on a dark brown mare, she trotted across the field, not heeding him. Chill morning air stung his throat and winter grass, sparkling with scattered diamonds of frost, crunched beneath his boots. Elizabeth should have been resting as the physician had instructed. Though he couldn't blame her for needing fresh air, since Joan had woken the household in hysteria again last night. His mother had slapped her face eventually, then stared in horror at her hand. The blow had worked: Joan had stopped screaming and allowed him to lead her to a chair and wrap her up warm. Huddled into a blanket, eyes wide and scared, it was easy to think of her as the young child she used to be, until she moved and the swelling of her belly showed.

Will's fists balled. Thankfully, Edmund was dead, else he'd have torn the country apart in pursuit of him. Poor Alice was still in bed, and last night Elizabeth's shaking as she suffered night terrors had driven straight into his heart.

The vegetation crunched under his boots as he strode across the field, then caught his breath. Elizabeth was trotting her horse towards a fallen tree. Surely she wasn't going to jump?

'Elizabeth, no!' he shouted.

She halted the animal, smiling. How could she be so reckless? Did she not understand that it would destroy him to lose a second wife? Turning her mount, she cantered towards him in the mist, horse and rider blending together into a single creature, a beautiful centaur belonging to the land. Bringing the animal to a stop front of him, she looked down, laughing.

'My lord,' she said.

'Let me help you down, my lady.'

He took any chance to touch her, and after her feet rested on the ground, he kept his arm around her waist. Braided into a bun, her hair sparkled under a net of gold thread and her cheeks were flushed red. Unable to resist, Will lowered his mouth to her soft lips, warming them with his kiss. Elizabeth moved back.

'People might see,' she said.

'I apologise.' He refastened her cloak. 'And you, my lady, should not be riding.'

'I am fine, it does not hurt.' She pulled a hood over her head and caught her horse's bridle. 'I usually walk about the estate in the morning, my lord. Would you care to join me?'

'Certainly.' He narrowed his eyes to look at the distant fields. 'Where are the sheep?'

'I instructed the shepherd to take them up the hill, it has better grazing.'

'And gets snowbound in winter.'

'It is not that cold yet, I was going to move them before Christmas.'

'They'll need to be moved today, the top fields aren't suitable.'

Her brow creased. 'You left me in charge, so don't criticise my decisions. And I don't want to go back to sitting in the solar either, now you are returned. I'm used to working.'

'So I have returned to find a mutiny on my hands?'

'If you wanted a wife who'd sit quietly sewing, then you chose the wrong one.'

'I don't remember there being a choice.'

Her face paled; he had hurt her. But what did she expect? Shorecross was his responsibility, and a heavy one, yet she thought herself capable of running it after only a few weeks. Didn't she understand how close to the line they were? One bad harvest, or poor wool yield, and his workers could starve. Their meagre savings wouldn't last long.

He pressed his lips tight. 'My land is not your duty.'

'Then what is my duty? Why am I here? You say you don't want to lose me, but our marriage is a sham!' She picked up the hem of her riding gown and hurried across the field.

Will watched her go. Better let her calm down. He needed time to think himself, because she spoke the painful truth. What future could they have? Catching the reins of her horse, he wound them around his hand, patting the spirited mare. Elizabeth would never be content with running just the house, like Joan. Like him, she needed to be outside. She was the perfect wife for him, but if he asked her to stay, it would be to deny her the chance of being a mother. If he got her with child, knowing what might happen, he would be little more than a murderer.

Was it right to encourage her to stay at Shorecross when he couldn't give her a family of her own? Shouldn't she be given the chance to live a full and normal life?

Sighing, he glanced at her horse. A

ride across Shorecross might help settle his thoughts. Putting his foot in the stirrup, he hoisted himself up and flicked the reins.

The yellow morning sun shone over the browning tops of parsnips left in the ground to harden off. Weeds were hoed and the ploughing completed. Elizabeth had done a good job, but instead of thanking her, he had dismissed her efforts. Flicking the reins of the horse, he squinted his eyes at a flash of crimson on the hill. It was her gown, always so visible. Galloping over, he looped the reins up, and strode towards her.

Elizabeth sat on her cloak on the frozen ground, a haze of mist rising from the frozen ground around her.

'Please stand up,' he said. 'You'll freeze.'

Elizabeth shook her head, keeping her face turned away from him. So he dropped down beside her instead, kneeling on the frozen soil.

'I'm sorry. You did a marvellous job

of running the estate and I should have been more grateful.'

She stared at the ground, sunlight glinting from her gold hairnet.

'Look,' he said, desperately, 'you can have part of the estate to run under your sole control. I won't interfere. What area would you like?'

She looked at him. 'Any part?'

'Yes.'

'I'd like the sheep.'

The sheep? He stared at the white dots on the hill opposite and his chest tightened. They were the most valuable part of the estate. Could he trust her?

Elizabeth sat silent beside him, and he smiled. She knew their value and was testing him. Yet he knew her well enough to realise she wouldn't risk the lives of his villeins by being careless.

'All right, the sheep,' he said.

Elizabeth nodded. 'I'll go and check on them now.'

He reached over to help her up, but she brushed away his hands and strode down the hill to the main fields. Will watched her go. He should apply for the annulment as he had promised, but couldn't bear to do it.

* * *

'Is everything well, Elizabeth?' Margaret said.

Elizabeth looked up from parchment she was reading. The lines of close writing were cramped and hard to read by the solar candlelight, but she had to be careful or Will would never let her touch his lands again. Knowing him as she did, it was a miracle that he had allowed her in the first place. The responsibility to his land and people would always come first.

'Elizabeth?' Margaret said.

'I'm fine.'

Her mother-in-law bit a piece of thread and held the garment up. It was a baby bonnet embroidered with white daisies. With a shiver, Elizabeth remembered the tiny bootees she had found in the desk drawer. Had Margaret stitched those too?

Glancing at the rain-lashed shutters, she pressed her lips together. Will hadn't come in yet. Should she go to him and apologise? But the lack of appreciation for the work she had done made her cross. How easy would it be to live the rest of her life with a man so obsessed by the land?

Margaret cleared her throat.

'Stand up to him, Elizabeth. He has had his own way too often.' She held the bonnet up again and pretended to inspect the stitching.

Elizabeth nodded. 'How is Joan?' she said.

'Not so well. She loved Edmund, and this has hit her hard. I hope she can recover before the child is born.'

'I've hardly seen her since that night. Every time I visit her room, she is sleeping.'

Margaret placed the bonnet in a wooden box. She straightened and looked at Elizabeth.

'I had to tell her about you and Edmund, since it was clear you had a history.'

Elizabeth went cold. She should have told her sister-in-law herself. Joan would have been so hurt to find out from someone else.

'I'd better go and talk to her.'

★   ★   ★

Alice came out of Joan's room with a tray. Elizabeth held the door open, then strode in unannounced.

Joan sat by the fire huddled in a shawl, the pale skin around her eyes purpled, and dark hair tangled about her shoulders. The shutters were still closed and smoke drifted from the fireplace, making her sister-in-law appear ghost-like. Elizabeth shuddered with a sudden premonition. The baby was due soon.

'What do you want?' Joan said.

'To apologise. I should have told you about Edmund: it was wrong of me to conceal it from you.'

Joan smoothed out her blanket. 'You don't need to be sorry, I know my brother well enough. It was he who stopped you telling me, wasn't it? His over-protection borders on the ridiculous! Did he believe I could not cope with the news?'

'We didn't want to upset you.'

'I'm an adult, and capable of dealing with upsetting news. You made me feel so foolish. I'd been waiting for him to come back to me, while he proposed marriage to another and then plotted to kill us both. I paid for his escape from prison! Do you think I would have done that if I had known? This never would have happened if William stopped treating me like a child.'

'At least you know Edmund did not prefer me, since he tried to kill me also.'

Joan stared at her and then laughed. 'That is true. And we Downes have never had much luck in marriage partners. With the exception of you, of course — my brother adores you.'

Elizabeth sat down and closed her eyes. Joan had spoken the truth; Will did shield them too much. He had taken the decision never to have another child, and because of it, he could never have a true marriage. But her life was her own, and she had the right to make her own decisions.

'I have been lucky with Will,' she said. 'But Edmund could be charming, I also fell for his lies.'

'In truth, I did not examine his personality far. I wanted to be wed and have children, so it was my own fault.'

'I suppose you don't see many people here at Shorecross?'

'We are isolated. I did have an offer of marriage when I was eighteen, but stupidly I panicked and refused.' Joan plucked at the fringe of her blanket. 'My parents' marriage was terrible, and William's first one almost destroyed him. It gave me little faith that mine could be any happier.'

'You are right to be wary. I also learnt from Edmund how dangerous it is to wed the wrong person. There is no way out if you make a mistake, since your husband owns you entirely.'

'The first man who asked me was a good man, but he did not ask again even though I hinted.' She looked down at her stomach. 'Now, my life is as a widow with my family, and I can't complain since it is of my own doing.' She looked at Elizabeth. 'Things are easier since you arrived, though. William is more relaxed, and Mother has someone else to talk to. She wearies my ears some days.'

Joan reached out to squeeze Elizabeth's hand.

'Bear with us, Liz. We can be a tricky lot to deal with, I know. But we all love you.' She let go and put her palms on the side of her chair. 'Could you help me up? I must eat.'

'Of course.' Elizabeth assisted her to stand.

Seeing Joan safely on the arm of a servant, she stopped by a window in the corridor and gazed through the leaded panes. Rain beaded on the glass and in the distance stretched the dark brown fields, ploughed into furrows ready for the summer seed. Resting her forehead against the cool glass, she sighed. Why did life have to be so difficult? She loved Will, had known it for certain when he returned home. But they could never have a true marriage.

In the courtyard below, the main gate creaked open and she frowned. Who visited Shorecross? Had the sheriff come to investigate Edmund's death?

A dozen soldiers marched through into the courtyard, this time standing straight and wearing livery. These were no hired mercenaries.

She raced down the corridor to Will's study and found him seated at his desk, reading a letter, the steward standing beside him.

'Men have arrived. In uniform,' she said, panting.

He stared at her.

'Who are they?' she said.

He placed the letter on his desk, a

slight tremble to his fingers. 'I suspect they're here for me.'

'Why?'

'I deserted against the wishes of Lord Henry Percy. I've been waiting for him to pay a visit.'

Her mouth fell open. 'Deserters are hanged! Why did you take such a risk?'

Will stared at her, lips tight. 'Why do you think?'

He strode out the room.

12

Elizabeth hurried across the courtyard after her husband. The group of soldiers stood by the well, pouring water into drinking flasks. They didn't appear to be in a rush to arrest anyone. Elizabeth glanced at Will, who stopped and laughed.

'Hugh! If you knew the years you'd put on me this morning.' Then he looked at the soldiers and his brow creased.

Elizabeth stared at the men's blood-stained bandages and exhausted faces.

'What happened?' Will said.

'We lost,' Hugh Conrad said. 'The Earl of Northumberland barely escaped with his life, and Henry Percy was taken prisoner. We made camp by Lochmaben Stone and the Scottish spearman drove us into the tidal waters.' He closed his eyes. 'The shore was black with drowned bodies, and the froth on the river stained red with blood.'

'How many did you lose of my men?' Will said.

'Twenty. I paid off the rest of your mercenaries and left them in Cumbria. They're hoping to join another battle, but personally I believe we should stay out of Scotland for now.'

'Why do they want to go back?' Elizabeth said.

'Because it is their job, my lady,' Hugh said. 'If they do not fight, they do not eat.'

'Has Henry Percy been ransomed?' Will said.

'Not yet, but I suspect he will be soon.'

Will looked at the exhausted soldiers. 'Stay here a while. I owe you that. Your men can bunk in the guardhouse and we have room for you in the solar.'

'I'd be grateful. We are tired.' He glanced at Elizabeth. 'And who is this lovely lady?'

'This is my wife, Elizabeth.'

'Wife? Honoured to meet you, my lady.' Hugh laughed. 'Now you've surprised me, Will. I never thought you'd marry again.'

'It was sudden.'

'I'm delighted for your good fortune. My lady, I am at your disposal.'

'Please, call me Elizabeth, we do not stand on ceremony so far from town.' She glanced back at the house: two faces were peering out the upstairs window. 'Come into the Great Hall for bread and mead. You must be weary.'

* * *

Elizabeth tied her cloak on and stepped into the courtyard, the frost crunching beneath her shoes. The door opened again behind her and Hugh came out.

'Elizabeth,' he said, bowing. 'May I accompany you?'

'Of course, but I am only going to check on the sheep. Have you settled in?'

'Very well.' He hesitated. 'I have not seen Lady Joan yet, even though I have been here overnight. Is she indisposed?'

Elizabeth remembered the face at the window. Joan couldn't hide forever.

'She is resting. Joan is with child.'

Hugh gave a sharp intake of breathe. 'I was not aware she had wed.'

'She is a widow, but we do not mourn her husband. He did not deserve her.'

'I hope he did not ill-treat her?' His hand went to his sword.

'She is safe here, with her family. We love her dearly.'

'Yes, she is easy to love.'

Elizabeth glanced at him. Was Hugh the man who had asked Joan to marry him? She would ask the girl later. Now, she had more important things to worry about.

'Did the Earl of Northumberland notice my husband had left?'

'I hope not. William took a huge risk in deserting. If Henry Percy had noticed, he certainly would have ordered him to be arrested.'

'He had no choice but to leave. Joan and I would have died if he had not returned when he did.'

Hugh paled. 'I understand entirely.'

Elizabeth took his arm as they strode across the fields. 'It's lovely to be out early in the morning. I must check on the sheep, then we can go for a stroll.'

Hugh raised his eyebrows. 'Marriage must have softened William. I never thought he'd let anyone touch his precious Shorecross.'

She smiled tightly. 'I must speak to the shepherd, we have three ailing sheep.' She strode over towards the waiting man, her long gown scraping across the frozen soil.

'My lady, do not get dirty,' the shepherd said, as she leaned down to examine the sheep.

'It is impossible not to in these gowns. I must get breeches like my husband.'

The man flushed and she grinned.

'Put the sick sheep in the barn for a few days, until we know what is wrong with them.'

Dusting her hands, she turned back to Hugh and caught her breath. Will stood beside his friend, the sun glinting from the strands of red in his dark hair. Her husband's face was pale and thick shadows circled his eyes. They now shared a bed together, but he did not touch her. He spoke civilly to her, but he moved away if she came near.

'My lady?' the shepherd said.

She looked down at the animal. 'Take her to the barn.'

Pushing back her hood, she watched the creature trot off. All the enjoyment had gone from farming; instead of bringing her and Will closer together, it had driven them further apart.

'Are the animals all right?' Hugh said, as she joined them.

'Yes,' she said. She did not want Will thinking she was not looking after them properly.

'It is an excellent wife you have here,

Will. Not many women would take on the land as well as the house.'

'My mother runs the house, so Elizabeth is not overtaxed.'

Her lips tightened. 'I must leave you, gentlemen. I have much to do.'

Swivelling on one heel, she turned and strode across the field, not caring if Hugh thought her rude. She meant nothing to Will now, not since he returned from Scotland. Was this his way of driving her from Shorecross? But it was a cruel method, and out of character. Always in their dealings, he had been honest.

Footsteps came from behind her and she paused, desperate to feel his hand on her shoulder.

'Elizabeth,' Hugh said. 'Are you all right?'

'I am fine.'

He took her arm. 'Give him time; the Downes family are a complicated lot. Will loves you, even if he doesn't show it.'

'He does not seem to care for me.'

'He is from a family of failed marriages. Not only did he lose Adela, but his father was a brute.'

'How long have you known Will?'

'We shared a tutor as boys. My family is comfortable, but not wealthy, and his father refused to pay much for his son's education. We learnt Latin and mathematics together for many years.' Hugh hesitated. 'A few years ago, I asked Lady Joan to marry me, but she refused.'

'She told me. And said you were a good man.'

'Did she?'

Elizabeth stopped. 'Joan wasn't ready to wed then, but things might have changed.'

'Thank you, I will see. You give me hope. I cannot offer her riches as fits her title, but I can give her love and a comfortable home.'

'I do not believe she has much interest in money.'

'And I do not believe she has much interest in me.' He smiled. 'I left last time a hurt man, but years bring understanding. And I don't mind her being with child; I like children. I just wish I'd known she felt ready to wed, because I would have returned to repeat my offer.'

'She was taken in by a charming man who treated her cruelly.'

'Yes, Will said. She hasn't emerged from her room since my arrival.'

'She is shamed for you to see her.'

'I do not care about her condition, so long as she no longer loves the other man?' He looked at her enquiringly.

'She doesn't. I'll try to persuade her from her room. It would be good for her to talk to you.'

'Thank you, that is very kind.'

Elizabeth smiled and turned to walk back to the house. She had never before been a matchmaker, and the irony of her helping two other hearts find love while her own lay broken did not escape her.

* * *

Will watched from his study window as Joan and Hugh strolled in the garden. A week ago, Elizabeth had led Joan from her hiding place and sent her for a walk with Hugh and her mother. Now, a morning stroll had become their habit, and with Margaret finding excuses to stay in the house, Joan and Hugh walked alone. Will glanced at their linked arms. He should tell them to move apart to guard Joan's reputation, but there didn't seem much point now, and Hugh was a respectable man.

Will raised his gaze to the fields behind them, until a flash of red caught his gaze, and he narrowed his eyes to watch Elizabeth stride over the furrowed earth. She had left their room early that morning as he dozed from a restless night. It was agony to sleep beside her, listening to her breathe, her warm body occasionally touching his as she moved. He had taken to rising early and going to bed late so he would not be tempted to touch her.

She had noticed the way he acted

towards her now; it was clear from the hurt look in her eyes, and he hated himself for causing her pain. But he had to let her go, else she would resent him for not being able to give her a proper marriage and family of her own. Elizabeth was everything he wanted, and would have made a wonderful wife. In order to ask for an annulment, he could only pull away and hope that, by some miracle, distancing himself would lessen the love he felt.

He could not cause the death of another woman.

★   ★   ★

'Elizabeth?'

'Are you all right, Joan?' Elizabeth swung her legs down from her bed. She had taken to resting in the afternoons to make up for the sleepless nights.

'Yes.' The other girl's face was bright and her cheeks flushed. 'Hugh is leaving tomorrow for his own estate.'

'That's earlier than planned.'

'He has news to tell his family.' Joan grinned. 'Oh, Elizabeth! He's just gone to ask William for permission to wed me. I know it is quick, but we have known each other for a long time.'

'Wonderful news! I'm delighted for you both. When is the happy day?'

'We will marry after the child is born.'

'But why? Does Hugh not want to take on the baby?'

'It is me who refused to marry him before.' Joan bit her lip. 'I did not want to risk him being a sudden widower.'

'It will not matter if you are wed or not, his pain will be the same.'

'It matters to me. And I have asked him to return home until we send word that my confinement is over, so he does not have to pace the study like my brother did, hearing his wife scream. William has promised to ride over with the news.'

Elizabeth held out her hand. 'You're scared, aren't you?'

Joan's eyes filled with tears. 'I heard

her too that night, screaming. But I still don't regret my condition. Remember that, Elizabeth; tell my family that. I regret nothing. They mustn't destroy themselves over another bad birth. I risked becoming pregnant with the full knowledge of what might happen.'

'Of course I will tell them.' Elizabeth embraced Joan. 'And I will be with you every minute of the labour. All we can do for you will be done. Then you will hold your baby in your arms and gaze at its tiny face, loving it with all your heart.'

Joan nodded, wiping her eyes.

Elizabeth smiled. 'Now, I think you must go and see Hugh off, before he comes in search of you.'

She dropped onto the bed as Joan's footsteps echoed down the hall. Wrapping her arms around the pillow, she pressed her face against it to breathe in Will's scent. Joan's happiness had made her own life seem even more desolate. She was willing to take the risk of becoming Will's real wife, but he'd made it clear that he didn't want her anymore. Now Edmund had gone, she was to be discarded.

Sighing, she stood up and reached for her cloak. A walk might help to cheer her up.

Stepping through the courtyard, Elizabeth leant against a waist-high stone wall and stared at the fields, sparkling with early evening frost. Behind them, a dark yellow sunset spread across the sky. Wrapping her cloak tighter over her shoulders, she watched her breath cloud in front of her. It was almost time to go into the Great Hall, to sit by her husband and stare at the empty plate in front of her as they both neither ate nor talked. Each night, she vowed to speak to him privately, but he came to bed so late she was too weary. There was no joy in him sharing her room anymore — she wished he would sleep elsewhere and save her the agony of having his back against her. Had it been her own home, she would have moved out of the room herself, but changing here would mean involving Margaret.

She sighed. In truth, there was little chance the sharp-eyed woman had failed to notice the situation between her and Will, but thankfully she kept her thoughts to herself.

Muted conversation drifted over, and Elizabeth turned to see her sister-in-law and Hugh striding along a path in the field beneath her. Lost in conversation, they failed to notice her, but Margaret, trailing behind as a reluctant chaperone, looked up and smiled.

'I am sure my presence is not necessary,' she said. 'I'll wait with you, Elizabeth, until they return.' She opened the gate and came through.

'They are close,' Elizabeth said, watching them.

'Yes, she would have been a fool to turn him down. In her position she cannot be picky.' Margaret rested her arms on the wall. 'I believed her ruined.'

'She is a respectable widow.'

'We can't prove she was married, and her brother killed her husband. It doesn't look good on the marriage market.'

'It is unlikely he'll do it again.'

Margaret smiled. 'I'm glad you came here, The house will seem empty when Joan leaves, although thankfully Hugh's family home is not far away.'

'I had not thought of her leaving us.' Elizabeth pressed her lips together. Of course Joan would have to leave, and the baby along with her. It brought a pang of sadness, since she'd been looking forward to having a child in the house. Though how long would she remain here herself?

'Does Hugh still plan to leave tomorrow?'

'Yes, Joan wishes it, although he would rather stay. He is a good man and suits her well. Perhaps it would have been better if I had made her marry him several years ago, but I have never been one for forcing my children to do things. My father pushed me into marriage, and I resented him for it when my husband turned out to be a violent drunk.'

'Did your family help you?'

Margaret shook her head. 'I was abandoned by the people who forced me to wed him! Such a cruel man. The happiest day of my life was when he fell off his horse, drunk.'

'Is that how he died?'

'Well, he might have survived with prompt medical attention, but it took some time for us to saddle an animal and find someone to ride for a doctor. By the time a kitchen maid had ridden back on a pack donkey with the physician, it was too late. My husband had bled to death.'

'A shame.'

'Yes,' Margaret said.

'Mother,' Joan called.

Elizabeth looked up at Joan and Hugh strolling towards them, arms linked. Joan, who had her dark hair bundled into a net and was wearing a deep pink gown, stepped with care along the mud path. Then the dinner bell pealed from the house, summoning the workers to come in from the fields, and Elizabeth sighed. It would be better to stay in the cold air than sit beside her silent husband.

'We must go, I am starving!' Joan said.

Elizabeth followed them, sitting slowly at the trestle table and washing her hands in the finger bowl. Her stomach rumbled but she had no appetite for the roast lamb.

'I will be sorry to leave tonight,' Hugh said.

'Yes, I shall miss you,' Joan said.

'Not long until I return, and then we can be wed.'

'Excuse my lateness,' Will said, striding across the hall.

'Were you held up in town?' Margaret said, pouring a cup of mead.

Elizabeth looked up, noticing the neat black and silver surcoat he wore — so different from his usual linen shirts. He had been out on a trip and not asked her to go with him.

'The price of wool is expected to be high this year, since the Flanders merchants are still buying all they can get their hands on. We will export in the spring,' he said.

Elizabeth looked at him. 'The sheep are my concern.'

'But still belong to me.'

'I'm not exporting *all* the fleeces; it is unfair to our local weavers.'

'Do not accuse me of treating my villeins poorly.'

'I was only saying . . . '

'A portion of the wool will be kept for the local market, as I have done every year for a decade! Before you arrived, madam, to tell me how to run my estate.'

Stung, she stared down at her plate, aware of the shocked expressions of his family and steward who sat with them. Cheeks flushed, she took a mouthful of wine, then pushed back her chair and rose from the table. Without another word, she strode out the room, head held high and her shoes clicking on the stone floor. But when she reached the circular staircase, she raced up the steps to her bedroom. This time he had humiliated her in public. It was time to leave.

13

Opening the chest, Elizabeth took out her spare dresses. Bundling the clothes up, she tied them into her cloak and added her hairbrush and writing tablet. As soon as Hugh left, she'd ask the stable boy to saddle her horse and leave.

Will mustn't know where she was going, else it would leave her in hope that he might come after her. Taking a deep breath, she wiped her eyes, the tears flowing freely now her anger had abated. She needed that anger back to remind herself of his behaviour, else she wouldn't be able to leave. How had they changed to being virtual strangers in such a short time? Had the deaths of Adela and his son left him too scarred to ever love again?

Remembering the tiny shoes, she choked back a sob. But Will had made it clear that he didn't want her around, and all she could do now was leave while she still had some dignity left. Grabbing a cloth bag, she made her way down the stairs to the strongroom, guarded by a single man with a short sword. He scrambled to his feet when she strode into the chamber.

'My lady,' he stammered.

'I'm here to collect some coin,' she said.

'How much would you like, mistress?'

'Only the money I brought here.' Crossing the room, she opened her dowry chest and filled the cloth bag. Hefting it, she took out a few pieces of silver, and put them back in the box to pay for her gowns.

'Elizabeth, Hugh is leaving!' Margaret shouted up the stairs.

'I'm coming down now,' she called back, then turned to the guard. 'I'll leave this bag here and collect it on my way back.'

'Certainly, my lady.' He bowed.

In the courtyard, Joan clung to Hugh's hand. Elizabeth swallowed and blinked. It would be hard to say goodbye to Hugh without crying herself. They would think her hopelessly overemotional. How could Will treat her like this, when she loved him so? But he didn't love her, and she couldn't stay somewhere she wasn't wanted. It would mean dying a little bit inside each day from his indifference towards her.

Joan wiped her eyes and smiled. 'I'll miss our morning walks, Hugh.'

'I would be delighted to stay,' he said.

'I don't want you to hear me in labour. I would be more settled in my mind if I didn't have to worry about you pacing the study beneath my feet.' Joan glanced at Will, who stood holding his friend's horse. His face was fixed, skin pale.

'Then I will return the moment I am summoned!' Hugh kissed her, then turned to bow to Elizabeth.

'Goodbye, my new sister, it has been

lovely to meet you,' he said. 'Please take care of Joan for me.'

Her mouth dried. She couldn't promise to look after Joan, or be there when she went into labour. It wasn't just Will she was leaving, but this entire family who had become dear to her.

Hugh swung himself up to his horse and trotted out the gate, hooves clopping on the hard earth. Joan sniffed and Margaret put her arms around her daughter.

'Come into the warm,' she said. 'You shouldn't be out here long in your condition.'

'It is not much warmer in the solar,' Joan said, but she followed her mother back into the house.

Elizabeth stepped into the stables and checked her horse. The animal nickered and she stroked its nose, remembering when it had just been the two of them at St Briavel's castle. It seemed such a long time ago now, and her stomach clenched at the thought of being alone again. Maybe she should return home to her uncle? Edmund was dead. But the thought of being under her aunt's tight control again made her shudder. She was too used to the freedom of Shorecross where she walked the fields as mistress, answerable only to her husband.

Giving the creature a last pat, she crept upstairs to collect her bags. As she went past Will's study, a chair moved against the floor inside, so she knew he had returned to work. There was no need for him to avoid their bedroom tonight; by the time he retired, she would be long gone.

* * *

Elizabeth put her bundle of clothes on the stable floor and cleared her throat. The painful lump in her throat made it hard to speak. Outside, the sky had darkened to navy blue, the dying light of the sunset touching the horizon. It wasn't the time for a woman to travel alone, but she had no choice. It wouldn't be possible to take a Shore-cross servant with her. Shivering, she wrapped her cloak around herself, and checked her money bag again.

'Can I help, my lady?' the stable boy said.

'Could you saddle my mount, please? And a spare pack horse, which I will have returned.'

He hesitated, looking at her bundle of belongings.

'You must not travel alone, my lady. The master would never permit it.'

'I'm not going far.'

He bit his lip, but reached for a saddle.

Elizabeth stepped back into the courtyard, and gazed at the dark entrance to Shorecross with a shiver. Where was she going? Would there be a convent in town? She'd be safe there. Looking at the house, she shook her head. So foolish to think he would search for her — that he cared for her still.

Picking up her bags, she glanced into

the stable. The lad was taking a long time. But the hut was empty, save for the horses and rows of shining tack, and her stomach clenched. The boy had crept out whilst she stared at the gate.

Loud, familiar footsteps echoed across the cobblestones, and she stiffened. The child had been to fetch his master, and now she would have to explain to Will what she was doing. Elizabeth raised her chin; she wasn't one of his workers, or even a true wife. He had no hold over her, and she could leave if she wished.

'What are you doing?' Will said.

She glanced at the stable lad and the youngster flushed, darting back into the stable.

'Are you insane? Do you know how dangerous it is to travel alone?'

'I'm not staying here any longer to be humiliated and ignored.'

He reached towards her, before appearing to check himself, and moved away again. Elizabeth pressed her lips together — it was clear he couldn't even bear to stand near her. She looked at him, head high, and he closed his eyes. It must be a trick of the light that made his eyes gleam as if they were filled with tears.

'If you wish to leave, then Robert will escort you,' he said.

'No, I'll be fine alone.'

'Take Robert, else I will lock the gate.' He pressed his lips together.

Elizabeth breathed in sharply, acid from her stomach filling the back of her throat with a sharp tang. Will was not going to ask her to stay. She had been right; he did not love her. Dropping her head down, she wiped her eyes. At least she had made the right decision; all she could do now was leave with dignity.

Will twisted away, striding across the courtyard into the stables. A few minutes later he emerged with two horses, bridled and saddled. It couldn't be any clearer that he wanted her to leave. However, instead of immediately boosting her onto the animal, he fussed with the creature, tightening the straps and checking the saddle again.

'Have you provisions?' he said.

She shook her head.

'My lord?' Robert called from the doorway.

'I need you to escort Lady Elizabeth. Collect your travelling pack while I get supplies from the kitchen.' He walked into the house.

Robert looked at her, brow creased.

'Where are we going, my lady?'

'Away from here.'

The man hesitated, then nodded, and vanished back inside. Elizabeth stroked her horse, hiding her reddened cheeks and tear-filled eyes against the creature's fur. Was all of Shorecross to witness her humiliation? Will strode out the manor house door with a large bag that he threw to the stable boy.

'Fasten to the pack horse, please.' He stopped and inhaled deeply, half-closing his eyes as if a sudden pain had hit him. Elizabeth moved forward instinctively, then held her ground. She was the last person he would want to comfort him. He was probably just relieved she was going.

'Are you all right, my lord?' Robert said, stepping into the courtyard, swinging a bag in his hand.

Will gave a curt nod, then motioned the man nearer. Elizabeth tilted her head to listen.

'Take her to the inn outside the village,' Will said. 'Do not go into the forest, it's too dangerous this time of night. Then take her tomorrow to her uncle.'

'It's my decision where I go,' she said.

He didn't look at her, just stepped back as the stable boy boosted her into the saddle. Hot tears burnt her eyes, and he glanced up, her gaze holding hers. She swallowed as she stared at his familiar chestnut eyes, remembering the nights they had spent in each other's arms, the kindness he had once shown. How could love vanish so quickly? Her cousin had told her that the opposite of love wasn't hate, but indifference. If that was true, then she knew his feelings towards her. She was nothing to him, worth less than the ducks on his pond.

'Goodbye, Will,' she said, her voice breaking.

He nodded.

Elizabeth turned her horse and walked towards the gate, Robert behind her. She glanced back over her shoulder once; Will stood in the dim courtyard, watching.

★   ★   ★

'Where has she gone?' Margaret said.

'Back to her uncle's, Mother. Now please leave me, I wish to be alone.'

To Will's relief, she stepped back and let him into the house. Racing upstairs, he stopped on the landing. It would be too painful to go into the room they had shared, to see her side of the bed empty. Inhaling hard, swallowing to stop the tears that threatened to spill from his eyes, he fumbled for the handle of his old chamber and flung back the door.

Alice stood in the centre of the room, a brush in her hand.

'My lord?' she said.

He cursed. 'Leave that for now, I need to rest.'

'Yes, sir.' Alice hesitated. 'Do you need anything, my lord?'

All he wanted was Elizabeth back, but he had to be strong, to let her go, so she could be happy. She would never understand why he had been forced to treat her as he did, since she hadn't heard the screams of Adela, or cradled the still body of a son in her arms. He couldn't risk Elizabeth dying; he loved her too much.

'Sir?' Alice said.

'Bring me wine, please. Two jugs.'

Alice raised her eyebrows, but left the door, closing the door behind her. Will pulled the heavy shutters down to stop himself staring out into the lane. He had to let her go, for he could not lose another wife and keep his reason.

Alice opened the door and quietly placed a couple of jugs on the floor. Will stared at them, breathing heavily.

★ ★ ★

Elizabeth trotted her horse up the road, cheeks wet with tears, longing for him to ride after them and beg her not to go. Blindly, she moved her mount to the side to allow Robert to take the lead.

'It's getting dark, my lady,' Robert said. 'We should think of finding an inn soon.'

She nodded sharply, not caring if they rode all night. There would be precious little relief in sleep tonight. Had she been alone, she would have just curled up under one of the trees, too desperate and heartbroken to travel further. Did love have to hurt this much? To leave such a raw pain that she couldn't ever imagine smiling again?

'My lady, we could return to Shorecross?' Robert said. 'Set off again tomorrow in the light.'

Elizabeth shook her head. She wasn't going back home to see Will's expression of exasperation when he realised she'd returned. Better to sleep under the trees in the mud than be humiliated again by him.

'Where is the inn?' she said.

'The other side of the village.'

'Let's go there then.'

Her horse stumbled on the dark path and she slowed the animal, staring ahead as the yellow lights of the inn appeared ahead. It had rough stone walls and a low straw roof, but at least it was away from Shorecross. As long as it had a bed she could huddle in to ease her muscles that suddenly ached unbearably.

'Stay here, my lady.' Robert said, sliding from his horse.

Looking up at the moon, she waited. Was Will already in his bed sleeping contentedly now she had gone? The tears she'd seen in his eyes must have been a trick of the light. Why would he cry for her?

Robert cleared his throat and she jumped.

'The inn is jammed to the rafters with pilgrims,' he said. 'But they've one room spare and a spot for me in the common room.'

She nodded, sliding wearily to the ground as the innkeeper's wife appeared in the door and dipped her knees. 'Pleasure to have you, my lady.'

'Thank you.' Elizabeth handed her reins to Robert and followed the woman into the taproom, filled with laughing, drinking pilgrims. The noise made her head ache and she longed to lie down on her bed, so she could hug the pillow and weep until her pain subsided.

'Up here, my lady.' The innkeeper's wife walked up a set of dark wood stairs. 'You're lucky, we've got our best room free. The pilgrims prefer to sleep on the floor and spend their pennies on ale.'

She pushed open a door. 'I'll be in shortly to light your candles.'

Elizabeth glanced at the single bedframe covered with grubby linen, and remembered lying in Will's arms in their warm bed at Shorecross, her head resting on his shoulder. Shaking her head, she went to the window and yanked the shutters closed.

Flinging herself on the bed, she stared at the ceiling. The bed was cold without him and she shivered. Had she done the right thing in leaving? She remembered his eyes again, more certain that it had been tears she'd seen. If he cared nothing for her, would he have organized food and sent Robert to accompany her?

True, he hadn't tried to stop her leaving, but it must have been a shock to him. She should have talked to him and explained why she was going. Instead, she had run away in a temper. She remembered the tiny shoes she had found and turning over, punched the pillow hard. Will had been damaged by the loss of his wife and child, blamed himself for their deaths. And instead of showing understanding, she had walked out. He had treated her poorly, but for the sake of the friendship they once shared, she should have spoken to him first.

Elizabeth sat up, head clear. She would return to Shorecross. The ride had given her chance to calm down and cool her anger. Will might not want to see her again, but she needed to explain her reasons for going, and find out why he had changed so suddenly towards her, else she would never forgive herself. She owed him that, at least.

★   ★   ★

Hooves clattered across the courtyard of Shorecross and the door to the manor house swung back. Margaret stood on the step, a lamp in her hand.

'Elizabeth?'

'Yes, it is me,' she said.

'I was very worried about you. Are you all right?'

Elizabeth swung down from her

horse and stepped into the welcome warmth of the house, reaching up to untie her dripping cloak.

'I am so glad to see you.' Her mother-in-law reached out for the garment. 'You must go upstairs immediately. William is drinking himself insensible.'

'What?'

'Just go to him, please, Elizabeth. He won't open the door to us.'

She ran up the stairs. Will never drank; he had told her he feared to do so in case he turned into his father. Had her leaving driven him to this? Reaching his door, she turned the handle, then hammered on it. No sound came from within. He wasn't used to strong drink. What if he had drunk so much it killed him? She banged on the door again, then stopped.

She still had the key to the connecting door. Darting in, she fitted it into the lock and swung it back, stepping quickly through his dressing-room to the chamber beyond. The darkness first hit her, then the musty, acid smell of red wine.

'Will?'

She peered into the gloom; then, crossing to the shutters, pushed them back to let the moonlight stream into the room. Will lay on the bed, head turned into the pillow, a drinking glass on the floor beneath him beside a puddle of burgundy wine which, for a frightening moment, she mistook for blood.

'Will?'

He groaned and turned away from her, coughing. Elizabeth jumped forward, waiting for him to be sick. But he just closed his eyes again and muttered.

'Elizabeth.'

'I'm here. I came back.'

Sitting on bed, she stroked his hair, the dark strands thick and strong in her fingers. A sheen of sweat covered his face and his linen shirt was rumpled. How much had he drunk? She glanced towards the door. Should she get Margaret? But he wouldn't want his mother to see him in this condition; he had intended for no-one to see him.

Rising from the bed, she poured a glass of water from a jug on the table and held it to his mouth. He choked, then drank thirstily. He would have a pounding head come morning. He dropped back on the pillow. Taking a blanket from the base of the bed, she covered him with it, her hands shaking. Tonight, she would share his bed one last time, and tomorrow they would talk.

Elizabeth pulled off her soft leather slippers and dragged her wet gown over her head. Climbing into bed beside him in her shift, she remembered the nights they had spent together. Now he lay drunk with his back to her, ignorant of her presence, yet hurt and possibly angry. Why did everything have to be so difficult? They were driving each other into despair. Turning against the pillow to stifle her sobs, she wept, desperate to find solace in emotional release, the way he had with alcoholic oblivion.

Elizabeth woke and winced at the painful cramp in her calf. Will lay with his leg thrown over hers, pinning her to the mattress. She smiled at the touch of his skin against hers, but the pain in her ankle flared again and she was forced to move.

'Elizabeth?' he muttered.

'Sorry. I didn't mean to wake you.'

Sitting up, she rubbed her foot, then narrowed her eyes to see in the dim light that came from between the shutters.

Will jerked upright. 'I thought you were a dream.'

'I came back to talk. However, you weren't capable of talking.'

'I'm sorry I treated you badly. I had hoped if I withdrew from you, I would love you less. You deserve children and a true marriage, and I cannot give you that.'

'I can cope with anything, except your coldness.'

He held her tight against him. 'Without you, my life has no meaning. You have the same thoughts and ideas I do. We match perfectly, but we have no future.'

'I have no future without you.'

He kissed her hair, stroking his hands down her shoulders.

'Do you want the annulment?' he said.

'Of course not. I have been dreading the day you would apply for it. I want to be here, with you.'

'Even when that means no children of your own?'

'We could adopt,' she said. 'There are many orphans in need of care.'

He slid his hands around her waist, but a loud hammering came from the door, and he straightened.

'You must come quick!' Alice shouted. 'Joan! It is Lady Joan!'

'The baby comes,' he said, grabbing his shirt and pulling it over his head.

Elizabeth grabbed her gown.

'Fasten this for me, Will?' she said.

He hastily did the back tie and pulled on his own hose and doublet.

'Alice?' Alice?' Elizabeth shouted, pushing her feet into slippers. 'Where is Joan?'

There was no answer. Will threw the door back and ran down the corridor, Elizabeth close behind, as a long and agonised scream came from the end of the hall.

14

Elizabeth threw open the door to Joan's chamber. Her sister-in-law sat on the edge of the mattress, her white chemise soaked in blood, her hand clutching the bedpost. As Elizabeth's mouth dropped open in shock, Joan bent forward and screamed.

'Come in, Elizabeth, quick,' Margaret shouted. 'William, you get out!'

'How long has she been like this?' Elizabeth slammed the door shut behind her.

'Not long, it came on so quickly.'

Elizabeth took a deep breath, nausea rising from her stomach. Joan looked like a woman who had been caught on a battlefield. How much worse could it get? Three of her cousins had given birth at her old home, and they'd spent the first few hours striding around the house muttering — and occasionally cursing — but on their feet and walking.

'Elizabeth, tell Alice to make up the fire and bring fresh linens. Send Robert for the midwife and physician,' Margaret said.

Elizabeth raced across the room and yanked the door open. A row of servants stood waiting in the hall, mouths open.

'Robert . . . ' she said.

'Lord Downes has gone to fetch the midwife,' Robert said. 'The kitchen's got the coppers on and Alice is fetching linen. What else can we do?'

Elizabeth stared at their pale faces, then closed her eyes as another scream came from the room. 'Pray. Go to the church.'

Robert's mouth tightened. 'Shall I send word to Mr Conrad?'

Elizabeth swallowed and remembered the dried flowers hidden in the drawer of Will's study. 'No, there is nothing he can do, and I would spare him this pain.'

Joan yelled, 'I can't do this, I cannot! Help me!'

Elizabeth swayed on her feet. She couldn't do this either. But she had promised Joan she would be there for her, and it was not the time for weakness. She shut the door and turned back to face the room. Joan lay crumpled at the end of the bed, her mouth twisted in agony.

'Tie the sheet, Elizabeth!' Margaret ordered, fastening a strong linen table-cloth to the nearest bedpost and throwing the other end towards her. Elizabeth wrapped the material around the bedpost, pulled it tight, then guided Joan's hands towards it. Immediately the girl grasped and pulled, screaming again as another powerful contraction cramped her womb.

A gasp came from the door, and Elizabeth turned to see Alice clutching a bundle of wood.

'Give it here,' Elizabeth said, reaching for the wood and lit taper. 'Go to the kitchen and get the cook to start making willow-bark tea.'

'I don't think that will help her,' Alice said. 'I helped my mother birth my younger brothers, and it wasn't like this! Oh, poor Lady Joan!' She shuddered.

'Go quickly, Alice!'

Joan screamed again and Elizabeth flinched. Thankfully, Will had gone for the midwife, and wasn't pacing his study listening to his sister's pain. She understood now why he had been so afraid of her becoming pregnant.

But then the door was flung back hard against the wall and Will stood there, wearing his riding clothes, with mud splashed up his boots. A middle-aged woman stood behind him, peering into the room, her face set.

'This is the midwife, Jane,' he said.

Dropping a large bag on the floor, he motioned the woman into the room. Elizabeth glanced over her shoulder as she placed a handful of twigs on the tiny flame in the fireplace. Jane wore a clean woollen gown and her hair had been braided under a spotless white coif. Already she was rolling her sleeves up, but the expression on her face was one of concern, rather than panic.

Leaning down to open her bag, the midwife said quietly, 'I'll need more help. This isn't going to be an easy birth.'

Will looked at Joan and his face paled. 'I've sent Robert to fetch the physician. Who else do you need? I can get midwives, priests — anything that will help. You must save her, my sister can't die!'

'I will do everything in my power,' Jane said. 'She is young and strong.'

'Out, William,' Margaret said. 'Wait downstairs, this is women's business.'

'Call me immediately if you need anything,' he said, stepping back and closing the door.

'Have her waters broken?' the midwife said.

'An hour ago,' Margaret said. 'Joan wanted a bath, but the pains started as soon as we got it filled.'

Elizabeth quickly rose from the fireplace and hugged her mother-in-law.

'She's going to be all right. Joan is young and strong like the midwife said.'

Margaret clung to her. 'So was I, so was Adela. Oh, Elizabeth, I know the pain my daughter suffers, and I know it will get worse! I can't bear it, I would rather it were me. To have to watch as she screams in pain! I can't lose her. She and William are my life. I have fought so long to protect her, but I couldn't save her from this — from the danger that all married women have to bear.'

Elizabeth swallowed the hard lump in her throat, tears in her eyes. She cringed as Joan screamed again. Her mother-in-law was right; it was easier to suffer the pain yourself then watch someone you loved endure it. How could Joan get through this? Taking a deep breath, she let go of Margaret and looked at Jane, who knelt beside her sister-in-law, examining her belly.

'How does it look?' she said.

The midwife pressed her hands to the swollen stomach, then smiled at Joan.

'A healthy, kicking baby! By nightfall he will be in your arms.'

Joan's shoulders slumped in relief, then she grabbed the tied sheet again and tensed. Jane stepped back to Elizabeth.

'The child is breech,' she whispered. 'It will not be an easy birth. She's bleeding heavily and the contractions are very strong. I fear for her.'

'Do what you can,' Margaret said. 'But I'll not lose my daughter. If we have to make a choice, save my girl!'

Elizabeth looked away from her mother-in-law's stricken face. 'I hope it will not come to that.'

'We'll do all we can. Let's get her up onto the bed,' Jane said.

Sweat dripped down Joan's forehead. Elizabeth took the girl's arm. 'We're going to move you, just a little.'

'Don't touch me!'

'We have to, you can't stay there,' the

midwife said. 'After this next contraction, lift her.'

Joan screamed, wrapping her hands
around Elizabeth's arm and gripping
tight. They hauled her up the bed,
resting her back against the pillows.

'Now, while I examine her, I want
you to hold her hands tight so she
doesn't move.'

Elizabeth clutched the girl tight in
her arms and stared down at the dark
hair, soaked in sweat, twisted into
clumps on the pillow. Would Joan
survive this?

★   ★   ★

Will paced the study, wincing at each
scream echoing through the silent
house. *Joan, Joan*, he thought, *I tried to
protect you from this. Damn you,
Edmund, I pray you are suffering for
what you have done to her!* He brought
his fists down hard on the table, then
turned away from the door. It was
women's business and he couldn't help.

He stared out the window. The sun had started to set so it had been eight, nine hours now. The times he feared, though, were when the shrieks stopped. How could she bear it? How could any woman go through this time and time again?

'My lord, they have requested a second midwife,' Robert said, appearing in the door.

'Then go and get one!' Will shouted.

'And the cradle.'

'Get Alice to fetch it.'

He drew in a sharp breath. If they needed the cradle, the baby must still be alive! Briefly, he thought of the baby for the first time. No children had been born alive at Shorecross since Joan. Closing his eyes, he remembered her as a young girl, his fellow companion in the nursery and equal sufferer of their father's rages.

He remembered the baby again.

Breathe, little one. Even though you are Edmund's child. Give her hope. Let this not have been for nothing again. Will strode to the fire and dropped to his knees in front of the grate. Putting his hands together, he started to pray.

* ★ *

Elizabeth sat on the pillow, holding her sister-in-law's hands. Joan groaned softly, head turned to the side.

'Have you tried to turn the child?' Elizabeth said. 'I have done it for lambs.'

'Too dangerous,' Jane said.

'More than bleeding to death?' Margaret said. 'She's not going to live much longer. Can you try, Elizabeth? Do you know how to do it?'

'For sheep. I did try it with my cousin, and the baby turned at the last minute.'

'Can you try? Please, Elizabeth?'

She looked at her sister-in-law, her white face on the pillow, sweating. The baby wasn't going to be born without help. There was no other choice.

'Margaret, I need you to hold her down.'

Elizabeth rolled up her sleeves and knelt down at the end of the bed. She

267

rested her head against the mattress and took a deep breath. Many times she had birthed lambs; but what if, rather than saving, she killed her sister-in-law? Was this the right thing to do?

Joan screamed again and Elizabeth straightened. She had no other choice.

★ ★ ★

Will sat on the floor, listening to every sound above him. It had gone silent and he feared the worst. Then the screaming came again, even louder, and his hands clutched the chair, knuckles turning white. Abruptly, the yelling stopped, and he closed his eyes. It was over. She was dead, like Adela.

Feet pounded down the corridor and Elizabeth raced into the room, her dress covered in blood, holding in her arms a bundle wrapped in white cloth.

'She lives, my lord, exhausted, but she should survive, and . . . ' She tilted the bundle in her arms. 'A boy, a healthy boy!'

Will looked into her shining eyes, remembering the fear he had seen there only a short time ago. Now she cried in joy, the pain she had seen in the birthing room forgotten. He watched her cradle the child, holding him in arms meant for loving, and a sick feeling rose from the base of his stomach.

'Would you like to hold him?' she said.

He shook his head.

'Then I must take him back, he needs to feed.' She looked back down at the child again.

'I'll come up.'

He followed her up the stairs and into the room.

'William, you can't come in here!' his mother said, looking up.

'I don't care that Joan has not been churched.'

The room reeked with a sharp, metallic scent; repulsive. He swallowed and looked at the pile of blood-soaked bedclothes and chemises lying in the corner of the room. Alice was on her knees scrubbing the floor, a bucket of murky water beside her. Joan lay in the bed, hardly visible beneath the pile of blankets, her face matching the snowy pillow beneath her head.

'It looks like a battlefield in here,' he said.

'That's exactly what it has been,' Margaret said.

Will leaned over the bed, wincing at his sister's bruised and bloody mouth, and when she half-opened her eyes again, he saw they were bloodshot.

'Will she be all right?'

'If fever does not set in.' Jane finished packing her bag. 'I'll stay until a nurse arrives, as Lady Joan has lost a lot of blood.'

'But she will survive?'

'She's young and healthy. She has a new baby to live for.' She straightened the bedclothes. 'The baby needs to feed. Has she organised a wet nurse?'

'She was going to feed him herself,' Elizabeth said.

'Well, she can't,' Margaret said. 'Go

down to the kitchen, Alice, and ask Marie to come. She's recently had a baby, and I'm sure she wouldn't mind feeding this little one for a few hours while Joan rests.'

Elizabeth peeled the baby off her shoulder and held him out to Margaret. For a moment, her mother-in-law stared at the baby, then reached over and took him in her arms.

'What a lot of trouble you've caused, little one,' she murmured.

'Have I time for a bath?' Elizabeth looked down at her gown, covered in crimson splashes.

'It would save shocking people,' Will said.

'Call me if Joan gets worse, or the baby is restless.' She leaned back over the child, touching his tiny face.

Will closed his eyes. Elizabeth loved the child already, that was clear. Would she really accept not having a child of her own?

Elizabeth stumbled and he reached out to support her.

'Lean on me, you're exhausted.'

He helped her back to their room, and she sank down on the stool as he ordered the bath to be brought in.

'I've seen quite a few births,' she said. 'But nothing like that. I thought she was going to die.' She opened her eyes and gazed at him, her expression soft and weary. 'But when I held the baby and he looked at me through those large blue eyes, I knew that I would still do it. Even after seeing that, I would risk having a child.'

'It's natural.' He knelt on the floor beside her and reached for her hands. 'But I can't lose another wife and child. I see no other result but death. There is no risk for me, only certainty.'

'There is not only death, though. There is also life, Will.'

He drew in a breath, surprised to find himself shaking. It had all been too much: hearing the screams again, then seeing Elizabeth without fear in her eyes. He was glad to be disturbed by the servants arriving with the wooden bath and buckets of hot water.

'Put it here,' he said, directing them to the window and watching them fill it.

'I must check on Joan and the baby,' Elizabeth said.

'No, you will not. It has been ten hours since she first went into labour, and you've not left that room since. You will bathe, eat and drink. Then after a rest, you can go and see Joan. You're no good to anyone if you collapse.'

'Marie is with the baby,' Alice said, from the door. She held out a pile of bath sheets.

Will took them off her and glanced at the girl's grey face.

'Go to bed, Alice, and rest. It has been a long day.'

'Thank you, sir.' She dipped her knee and hurried out the room.

Will pushed the door shut behind her and draped one of the bath sheets over the tub to line it. He swirled the hot water with his hand, then helped Elizabeth to her feet.

'Turn around,' he said. As he untied

her gown, she slumped against him; leaning down, he put his arm under her knees and lifted her up into his arms. Carrying her, he lowered her into the bath.

'Stay awake,' he said. 'I don't want you to drown.'

She smiled, raising a hand to wash the blood from her face.

'Let me.' He took a cloth from the pile Alice had brought in and rinsed it out. With gentle strokes, he smoothed it over her forehead and cheeks. She closed her eyes and relaxed into the hot water. Reaching down, he soaped her neck and breasts, resisting the urge to kiss her and caress her with his hands. Her head dropped back against the bath and she closed her eyes. He put his arm under her shoulders.

'Time to get out.'

Elizabeth rose to her feet, stumbling as she climbed over the edge of the bath. He wrapped her in the warmed bath sheet and laid her on the bed, pulling the blankets up to her chin. Leaning down, he allowed himself one kiss on her soft lips before he pulled the shutters across and left her to sleep.

15

Standing in Joan's chamber, Elizabeth looked at the sleeping baby held in her arms, breathing in his sweet scent. The tiny eyes lashes rested on his cheek and he opened his eyes briefly, before drifting back to sleep. Hugging him tight, she smiled; then the smile faded and she sighed. Rain rattled against the window and she moved to sit closer to the fire.

'Are you all right?' Margaret said. 'Tired?'

'I'm fine.' Elizabeth yawned, glancing at the bed where her sister-in-law lay still. She was certain Joan wasn't actually asleep; but, only a week after the birth, neither could she accuse the girl of pretending. A mewing cry came from the baby and she rose to her feet, walking over to the bed.

'Would you like to try feeding him?' she said.

Joan kept her eyes closed, until she clearly realised she wasn't fooling anyone, and then opened them.

'Not yet,' she said. 'I don't feel up to it. Take him to Marie.'

Margaret tutted and stood at the bottom of the bed. 'You're going to lose your milk if you don't feed him more often.'

'I don't care. I feel too ill. I can't cope with him.'

'Joan, he is your child, and you've hardly even held him.'

Joan turned her head away, tears sliding down her cheeks. 'Could you get me a cup of warm mead, Mother?'

Margaret sighed, but strode out the door.

'I could put the baby beside you on the bed?' Elizabeth said. 'And he must be given a name soon.'

'Ask Mother to think of one.'

Elizabeth went still, then sat on the side of the bed and touched her sister-in-law on the shoulder. 'Joan, please. I know you suffered. It's not his fault, though. Remember the love you had for him when he was in your belly.'

Joan propped herself up on her elbow. 'I do remember, which is why it terrifies me that I feel nothing for him now.' Putting her hands over her face, she sobbed, 'I feel nothing! He could be anyone's child. I don't want to hold him, I don't want him anywhere near me.'

Elizabeth drew in a sharp breath. It was worse than she feared. She looked down at the child in her arms, hugging him. How could anyone not fall in love with him? She had been looking after him for a week now, and he had woven himself tight into her heart.

Joan clutched Elizabeth's arm, her nails digging in. 'Can you adopt him?'

'What?'

'You and Will would look after him better than I would.'

Elizabeth stared at Joan. 'I don't think that's a good idea. He's your son.'

'He's more your son than mine. Every time I look at him, I remember the blood, the pain, the conviction that I was going to die. I don't love him, I feel nothing for him. He doesn't deserve that.'

'It's all right, Joan. I understand, I really do. Will has seen this reaction on the battlefield — brave men suddenly refusing to leave their tents, shaking at the sight of their armour. He thinks it's due to shock. And you had a terrible time during the birth. But don't lose your baby, because you'll regret it, I know you will. When you carried him inside you, you loved him.'

'But I don't now.' Joan lay back against the pillows, her cheekbones sharp and eyes shadowed. 'Please take him, Elizabeth. I'm scared of him, it upsets me to be near him.' Her voice broke and tears streamed down her cheeks. 'I'm such a bad mother. I should love my child. I don't feel it, though. I don't look at him in tenderness. I just want the crying to stop.'

Elizabeth moistened her lips and remembered a maidservant at home who had smothered her child. She hadn't loved the baby either. A week ago, she'd never have considered that Joan might do such a thing, but she'd known women react in strange and worrying ways after giving birth. She looked at the swaddled form in her arms.

'Could you just hold him while I go to check the sheep? I haven't been out the house all week.'

Joan closed her eyes. 'Could Mother take him?'

'She has to see Cook about the meals.'

Joan remained silent, arms stiff by her side. Elizabeth hoisted the baby against her shoulder, nestling him warm and soft against the skin of her neck. How could his mother not want him? Wearily, she rocked him as he began to cry. He did not even have a name yet, even though he was almost a week old. Joan should at least choose that for him.

'He must have a name,' she said.

'I don't know.' Joan turned her head away.

'You were thinking of Francis?' Margaret said, walking into the room, carrying a jug of mead.

'Yes. Francis,' Joan said, without interest. The baby began to cry and she shuddered.

'Take him away please, Elizabeth, let her rest,' Margaret said.

Carrying the baby, Elizabeth went back downstairs. When she had suggested the baby's cradle was put in her room, she'd not expected it to remain there for so many days. She yawned and used her free hand to rub her eyes. Luckily, Will was a deep sleeper, and further down the corridor, a room had been given to Marie while she was wet nursing. During the night, by candlelight, Elizabeth sat on a stool in Marie's room and watched her nurse, before taking the baby back to his cradle and rocking him to sleep.

She was thankful to have no other work except the sheep, for her mind was a permanent fog and her eyes gritty from lack of sleep. Margaret was too concerned about her daughter and busy running the house to care for the child, and it would be risky to trust a rabbit to Alice.

Today, it was a problem, though. She absolutely had to check on the flock and speak to the shepherd, but sleet drummed hard on the windows and a cold chill blew down the corridor when the front door was opened. She could ask Will to look at the sheep, but her pride prevented her. Sighing, she rested her elbows on the window sill and squinted out across the fields.

* * *

Will closed his ledger and frowned, peering through a gap in the door of his study at Elizabeth slumped by the window. It had been almost a week since she'd left the manor, and Elizabeth didn't take well to confinement.

'Are you all right?' he called.

She turned. 'I need to have a word with the shepherd, but . . . '

He looked at the baby.

'Can Joan take him?'

'She is not well. Marie is resting, and Alice . . . well, I wouldn't be sure.'

'Don't give him to Alice, she broke my inkwell last yesterday. Took an hour to clean up.' He cleared his throat to offer to check the sheep himself, then noticed the appeal in her eyes.

'Shall I take the baby? I can carry him around the room in the fashion you do.'

'Thank you. He is called Francis now.'

'Good choice.'

She held Francis out and Will took him. It was surprising how light and fragile the infant was.

'I won't be long,' Elizabeth said.

'Keep him warm, and if he needs a clout change, wake Marie.'

'I'm sure I'll manage, it can't be much different to caring for a young lamb.'

She hurried out the room.

Will placed the baby on his lap. 'Soon you'll be sitting at this desk to learn the trade. We'll get you a little writing desk to practice your letters.'

Francis blinked and Will smiled. The child's eyes were turning chestnut brown.

'There's no Edmund in you,' he said, in satisfaction.

The tiny mouth twitched.

'Are you smiling at me?'

He lifted the child up, breathed in a mixture of soap and the lavender scent of Elizabeth's perfume. For the last week he'd stayed away from the baby, afraid it would bring back memories; but, holding him now, he felt only love. How wonderful it would be to have a child of his own. To walk about Shorecross with his son or daughter holding his hand.

Elizabeth trudged back into the manor house, her hair wet from the icy rain. Shivering, she pulled her cloak off and went into Will's study.

'Is the flock all right?' he said.

'Yes.' She smiled. Francis lay asleep against his chest, a wet patch spreading on her husband's blue doublet as the baby dribbled in his sleep. 'Has he fed?'

'Marie has nursed him, although I had some trouble persuading her to return him. He's a dear little thing.'

Elizabeth touched the tiny hand and smiled as the fingers bent to grasp hers.

'Have you written to Hugh yet?' she said.

'I have. Joan told me not to, but I ignored her. She needs his support. And I fear she will never care for her baby until she is in her own home with him.'

'I don't think Joan should take Francis away until we know she is capable of caring for him.'

'She'll manage. I know at the

moment she's upset, but they just need time together. The cradle should be taken back to her room.'

'We need to be certain that Francis will be safe. I've known women act out of character after childbirth.'

'Joan wouldn't harm her baby.'

'But she doesn't love him and refuses to hold him. Francis could grow up starved of affection.'

Will's lips tightened and she remembered his own childhood. Then he glanced at the desk drawer that held the shoes of his own son — the child that never breathed.

'I know what it's like to lose a child,' he said. 'My sister doesn't deserve to feel that pain too.'

Elizabeth lowered her head. 'You're right. I must take him to her.'

'Let me hold him a moment longer.' He looked at her. 'You told me you would be willing to take the risk of childbirth.'

She caught her breath. 'I would.'

'You were right, there's also life in

childbirth. Seeing Francis has made me realise that. If you are willing to the take that risk, then so am I.'

Her eyes filled with tears and she reached down to hold him close, the baby between them.

'We can have a future,' she said.

'You are my future. I never wanted anyone but you.'

She touched her lips to his, then drew back, her tears falling onto the sleeping face of the baby.

'I had better get him back to Joan,' she said.

'Hold him close,' Will said, lifting the baby into her arms. 'He's very precious.'

Smiling, she walked slowly out of the study and along to her chamber, clutching the baby close. Pausing, she kissed his warm head. How wonderful it would be to hold her own child in her arms! And, even more delightful, she and Will could have the same marriage as other people, with a shared connection rather than this gap between them where their views differed so dramatically. With such a huge obstacle between them, it would have destroyed their relationship in the end.

As she passed Joan's room, the unmistakeable sound of sobbing came from behind the closed door, and Elizabeth shook her head. Will was right: Joan couldn't lose her child. She gave Francis a last, tight cuddle, before pushing the door to Joan's room open.

Her sister-in-law lay on the bed, eyes closed.

'I'm going to see the sheep, so Francis will need to stay with you for an hour or so,' Elizabeth said.

'No, please Elizabeth, I can't look after him! Don't leave me with him!' Joan sat up straight.

Elizabeth set her lips together. 'He is fed, changed and asleep. I'm going for a walk across the fields and your mother is resting. You don't have to do anything, but he's staying in here for the next hour until I've finished my work.'

'You're as bad as my brother! Nothing but Shorecross matters!' Joan said.

Elizabeth closed the door behind her, the unfairness bringing tears to her eyes. Too fearful to leave the landing, she sank down onto the floor outside Joan's chamber and rested her head back against the wall.

A whimper came from the bedroom and she sat up. There was a pause, then Francis started to scream and Elizabeth pressed her hands to her ears. Standing up, she reached for the door, then turned and walked down the hall instead, away from the crying. Striding the length of the corridor, she paused against outside the chamber, then made herself walk again. Francis would not come to harm from crying for a few minutes. Swallowing, she stood at the window, gazing out and remembering the tiny bootees in Will's drawer. Joan's pain of losing her child would be no less. She would have to watch from afar as her own flesh and blood rejected her in favour of Elizabeth. The harm caused would be too great.

The shrieks grew louder and she grabbed the doorknob, then heard a sound within and stopped. It was Joan's voice, speaking softly. Francis cried louder, then came the familiar squeaking of the cradle. Joan was rocking him. She stepped back from the door and walked to the stairs, smiling.

16

Elizabeth pushed the cradle into the shadows under the solar window, before sitting down. She glanced at the cradle, eyes bright. Would she soon have her own child in there? Joan's embroidery lay over the chair arm and she picked it up to sew a few stitches. Stabbing herself in the thumb with the needle and sucking her finger, she put the sewing back down. A rattle of hooves sounded in the courtyard outside and she rose to her feet. Had Hugh arrived?

'Soldiers,' Margaret said, looking out the window.

Elizabeth peered through the glass. A large group of armed men, mounted on horses, had ridden into the courtyard. Alice stood by the well and one of the soldiers leaned over to speak to her. She let go of the rope, and the bucket shot down the well as the maid raced back inside the house.

Elizabeth stepped back from the window, her chest tight as she remembered Will telling her about his desertion in Scotland. Running to the door, she wrenched it open as feet pounded up the stairs and Alice, her hair pulled from its net, raced up, panting.

'The master!' she said. 'They've come for the master.'

'Who are they?' Elizabeth said.

'Northumberland's men. They're here to arrest him. Mistress, what do we do? They can't take the master!'

Elizabeth stumbled and caught hold of the doorjamb to steady herself. It had to be because of Scotland. He had deserted to save his family from Edmund, and now the soldiers had come for him. Surely they would not hang him? No, they could not do that to Will; she would not let them! She ran down the stairs, Margaret and Alice pounding after. Robert hurried in the manor house doorway, mouth open.

'Lord Downes has been arrested,' he said. 'I couldn't stop them. He ordered me not to.'

Picking up her skirts, Elizabeth ran into the courtyard and across the fields. The group of soldiers was riding towards her, hard hooves kicking the ploughed furrows into the air. Winter sun glinted from their helmets and swords, their eyes set and menacing.

'Will?' she shouted.

A horseman stopped in front of her.

'What have you done with my husband?' she demanded.

The man pointed and she gasped, a hand to her mouth. Lord Downes had been bound to the back of a horse, sitting upright, but with his head dropped down low against his chest. Patches of crimson blood stained his shirt, dripping from his lowered face.

'Stay back, my lady!' a soldier said, kicking his horse to block her way.

'I have to see my husband.'

Will raised his head. The flesh of his face was bruised and bloodied, dark

293

brown eyes glazed and unfocused. Her eyes dropped to his waist. He wore no sword belt. Since Edmund's death, Will no longer went armed into the fields. Elizabeth stepped past the mounted soldier in front of her, but he lashed his horse backwards and stopped her again, this time drawing his sword.

'He's injured,' she said. 'Let me see to him!'

The soldier raised his sword higher and she stepped back.

'Please,' she said. 'I have no weapon.'

The man lowered his blade slightly, then lifted it again as a voice shouted across the field behind them.

'What have you done to my son?' Margaret yelled.

Elizabeth cursed under her breath.

'He is arrested for desertion. Treason.'

'My son's no enemy to the king! You are mistaken!' Margaret said. 'Let him go, immediately.'

'I have orders to take him to the Tower of London.'

Elizabeth gasped. The Tower of London? She'd heard of the horrors carried out there — torture and death, men crammed into tiny unheated cells to starve as they waited to hear their fate. Will couldn't be subject to that, not when he had deserted to save her from Edmund.

She stared at her husband and he shook his head.

'Let them do their job, Elizabeth,' he said. 'There is nothing you can do. Write to my lawyer and tell him where I am. He'll get me released, I am sure.'

Elizabeth shook her head. It would be impossible to stand by and watch them drag him away, bound and injured.

'I beg you,' she said, to the solider. 'Take me too.'

'No, my lady, orders are for Lord Downes only.'

'I'll follow on my own horse then.'

'Elizabeth, stay here,' Will said. 'There is nothing you can do. Write to my lawyer, but do not follow.'

She opened her mouth to protest, then turned at the sound of heavy footsteps behind her. Robert hurried across the field behind her, a money sack in his hand.

'No further,' a soldier warned him.

Lips pressed tight, Robert unbuckled his sword and laid it on the floor.

'I've got coin for Lord Downes, to pay for his food and comfort.'

The captain beckoned him over, took the bag and trickled the money through his fingers.

'All right,' he said.

'Lady Downes, Dowager Margaret Downes and I have all seen him being given this gold,' Robert said. 'And if it is missing when he reaches London, we will accuse you of theft.'

'He'll have the money. My men aren't thieves.'

Robert tied the bag to Will's belt and then squeezed his arm.

'Take care, sir, we'll get you out.'

Will raised his head again, and

Elizabeth shivered as she gazed into his blackened and swollen eyes. There was no way she was staying at Shorecross. They'd have to chain her to the barn doors first!

'I'm coming too. Please fetch my horse, Robert,' she said.

'My lady,' the soldier warned, 'if you're going to be difficult, remember that we hold your husband in custody. He can have an easy ride to London, or we can chain him and force him to walk. It is up to you.'

Will swayed in his saddle, and Elizabeth bit her lip. If they hadn't tied him on so tight, he would have fallen. There was no way he could walk.

'We're going to get you out, Will,' she said.

He blinked and narrowed his eyes to gaze at her. 'Northumberland is too powerful and you risk making yourself a dangerous enemy.'

'I believe the earl needs money for a ransom. He might accept payment in return for your pardon.'

'That'll take more cash than we have.'

'He'll take land. We could break the entailment?'

'Not Shorecross, Elizabeth. Promise me you'll never give him that! You would be handing over a living estate peopled with my tenants. I can't let them fall into the hands of an unscrupulous landowner. They're my responsibility.'

'What about your duty to me as your husband? Am I not owed a degree of care?'

'Don't do this to me, Elizabeth. It is unfair. I love you, but I don't live in a world with you alone. I've responsibilities, and can't sacrifice the lives of my people to save myself. Shorecross has an heir, and you and my mother can run the estate until Francis is old enough.' He looked into her eyes. 'I'm not my father, Elizabeth. If I sold my people, I would become him.'

'I can't bear to lose you.'

'You'll only lose me if you exchange

Shorecross for my life, because that would destroy me. Promise me you won't do it?'

Elizabeth closed her eyes, tears sliding down her cheek.

'I'm going to save you.' Her voice was low.

'Step back, mistress,' the soldier ordered.

Eyes stinging with angry tears, she moved away, twisting her hands together in anguish as the small party rode across the fields to the gate. Her husband glanced back over his shoulder, then his head dropped down again.

Picking up her skirts, Elizabeth raced into the manor. Now she had to act fast if she was going to see her husband again. The Tower! A place renowned for disease and death.

Footsteps echoed behind her. 'What do we do?' Margaret said, panting. 'How can we save him?'

'Money. We need to buy his freedom. Lord Northumberland's son is being held by the Scots; he'll need to raise a ransom.'

'We have little coin.'

'I know. Can we sell Shorecross?'

Margaret stopped. 'William would never allow it. He'd never sign the papers.'

'Could you?'

'He would never forgive you for it.'

'But he would be alive.'

'For what life, Elizabeth? What man would he be without the land that he loves, the people he cares for? I know my son — ' Her voice softened. ' — and so do you. There must be another way.'

'Then we need to sell the livestock, all the harvest. Everything on Shorecross. My jewels, our clothes. It must all go.'

'That we can do!' Margaret raised her skirts. 'I'll send messages to our friends, begging for loans. Write to Hugh, see if he can help.'

★　★　★

Seated at Will's desk, Elizabeth put her quill down and looked at her list of figures. Her husband had agreed she could offer the Earl of Northumberland two farms with protected tenancies, and she'd had the gold in the strongroom counted. Half the sheep flock was sold, and some of the cattle.

'It's not enough money,' she said.

Rising, she poked the fire, then held her chilled hands to the flames. Her husband had no fire, and this evening he would be pacing a narrow tower room with his breath freezing in the winter air. It was so unfair that he should suffer for Edmund's vengeance.

There was a knock on the door.

'My lady, you have two visitors,' the servant said, glancing in.

Elizabeth twisted around. Who could it be? Was it Northumberland, or a guard from the Tower bringing bad news? But the familiar figures of Uncle Walter and Hugh appeared in the doorway. Elizabeth raced across the room and into her uncle's arms.

'My dear girl.' Uncle Walter held her tight.

'We met en route,' Hugh said, unfastening the brooch of his mantle and draping the wet cloak over a chair. His boots left mud trails on the floorboards. 'I have come straight from the Tower. William is well and in good spirits.'

Held by Walter, Elizabeth breathed in the smell of sweat and horses — a male scent that left her dizzy with memory. She cleared her throat and stepped back. Hugh yawned and rubbed his hands together over the fire. Elizabeth looked at his whitened skin, stretched taut over sharp cheek-bones. If Hugh, veteran of dozens of wars, was afraid, then Will's situation was bad indeed.

'What are his lodgings like?' she said. 'Is he chained?'

'No, but the room is cold and unfurnished. I've asked the guards to move him and offered money. Keeping him alive is our first priority. He cannot die of gaol fever while we negotiate his release.'

Elizabeth shuddered.

'He's a strong man, but that place would test the constitution of a boar.'

'Has he enough food?'

'They're giving him black bread. However, he can't eat it as his mouth is still bruised. I arranged for a servant to stay with him. How do your negotiations for his release go?'

Elizabeth frowned. 'Tomorrow Northumberland's steward is arriving here to hear our offer. However, I fear the earl won't be reasonable while his son remains a prisoner of the Scots.'

'Yet we must free William before Henry Percy, since it is he whom Will defied.'

She shuddered. There had been too much vengeance lately.

He touched her shoulder and bowed. 'We'll get him out, I promise.'

Elizabeth nodded and watched them leave the room. If only she could be so easily comforted by Hugh's words, for in truth, her husband was in a desperate situation. Crossing to the window, she stared at the remaining sheep, which were already marked for sale. A thought nagged the back of her mind and she frowned, turning back to stare at the large ledgers of Shorecross. Why did it feel that she had missed something? Will had no other assets she could find.

* * *

Elizabeth pressed her lips together as Northumberland's steward sat on a bench in the main hall, while he read the letter she had given him. Did he have to take so long? The words were clear enough and she had always been praised for her neat writing. Beside her, Hugh stood still with his face expressionless. She wished she could master the expression since the steward seemed to be enjoying her discomfort.

Finally, the man screwed up her parchment.

'It's not enough. My master will only drop the charges in return for the main estate of Shoretree.'

'Shorecross,' Elizabeth snapped. 'And he can't have the land since my husband isn't able to sanction it.'

'The estate is entailed,' Hugh said.

The steward scratched his ear. 'The land of a criminal passes without encumbrance, so the entailment is of no concern.'

Elizabeth smoothed out her letter, fighting the urge to bang her fists on the table. She couldn't sign over Shorecross as it would destroy her husband. Will was quite capable of self-destruction. She cleared her throat.

'We're offering two farms with tenants and five hundred pounds in cash.'

The man stretched. 'Is Lord Downes aware that he is to be hanged? This isn't a time to negotiate.'

'Since he is locked in the Tower, I do believe he has noticed the seriousness of his position.'

'I'll write to my master with your offer and recommend that it is rejected. Now, I bid you goodbye, my lady, sir.'

'But . . . '

'Let him go, Elizabeth,' Hugh said. 'There's nothing else we can do.'

She turned to the steward. 'My husband is a good man who has done nothing wrong! Lord Downes doesn't deserve to be hanged because he protected his family.'

'Lady Downes, it has nothing to do with me.'

Elizabeth strode out the room and slammed the door hard enough to make the frame rattle.

'Odious man!' she said.

'No good?' Margaret said, from where she waited by the stairwell. 'He won't release my son?'

'We need more money.'

The other woman spread her fingers helplessly. 'There is no more. What else can we do?'

'I do not know.' Elizabeth sank to the floor and rested her head back against the panelling. How she missed her husband! He couldn't die, he simply couldn't.

'Have we been through every account book?' her mother-in-law said.

'Many times. There is not an asset I haven't sold or put on the market. The only thing left is the land itself.'

Margaret lowered her gaze. 'Do you think we could persuade William to sell? Is it worth a try? We are now that desperate.'

'You didn't want to before.'

'I've had longer to consider his fate. But I know we risk destroying him.'

'There must be another option.' She closed her eyes, rows of figures dancing through her exhausted mind. Her thoughts went back to the sheep. They were the most valuable item on Shorecross whilst the price of wool was so high. Sheep farms were selling at record prices. Could they sell part of the land?

With a sharp breath, she straightened, eyes wide.

'Margaret, I've been such a fool!'

'Elizabeth?'

She leapt to her feet. 'I hope it is not too late.'

'What *is* it?'

Elizabeth looked back over her shoulder. 'My land! I have sheep farms in Devon. I thought them worthless, but they can't be. Edmund was ready to kill for them. They must have a much higher value than I realised. Will's lawyer was going to look into them for me. I wonder if he has. How quickly we could get them valued?'

'They would take a while to sell, though. Would we have long enough?'

'They don't need to sell. The earl would accept land. We just need a value. Quick, call a messenger. We must get lawyers immediately to Devon.'

Margaret turned to run, then looked back. 'And it is yours to sell? We mustn't promise what we do not own.'

'It is mine, from my mother. It was designed to be my dowry; now it will be used to save my husband. Run,

Margaret, send messengers. I must stop the steward and ask him to remain here for another few days.'

Elizabeth raced through the main hall and into the courtyard. On a horse, the steward and his servants were trotting out of the gate.

'Stop!' she shouted. 'Please stop! We have more money.'

The man paused and slowly turned his horse, before smiling.

'There is always more money found, mistress. It's amazing what the power of the hangman's noose can bring out from under the floorboards.'

★ ★ ★

Were the farms worth enough? Elizabeth looked down at the letter from the lawyer again. He had valued them at half the price of Shorecross itself, an incredible amount of money for plain fields. Prime grazing land, apparently. Taking a deep breath, she knocked on the door of the room she had allocated to Northumberland's steward.

The man's servant opened the door on the third knock. Elizabeth shifted uneasily from one foot to the other as she stared at the man's face. Had she made a huge mistake? Should she have ignored Will's wishes and handed over Shorecross?

The servant cleared his throat.

'I need to see your master,' she said.

A man stood up behind a large desk, a quill in his hand and his eyes narrowed. 'Come in, Lady Downes. I knew you would come to your senses. Have you the details of the Shorecross estate?'

'I am not offering you Shorecross. There is an heir.'

His lips pressed together tightly. 'So you intend to keep the land for your son and let his father hang? Oh, lady, I'm glad you're not my wife.'

'I am here to plead his case, am I not?' Her hands trembled and she pushed them under her mantle. The man had to believe that the offer she

310

was making was the final one. She put a piece of parchment on the desk.

'This is our compensation payment in exchange for Lord Downes' freedom. It includes my land in Devon.'

'So you weren't going to offer that immediately?'

'I forgot about it.'

'Then you must have too much land.'

'That is all I have, there is none other.'

He picked up it, glanced at her sharply, and then hissed between his teeth.

'Your husband deserted a battle.'

'One man could not have turned the tide of war. And my husband didn't desert to save himself, but his family who were in grave danger.'

'That's of no concern to me or the earl.'

'Would you let your own son die?'

'If my duty demanded it.' But his mouth tightened.

Elizabeth moistened her lips. 'I have an extra fifty pounds from a friend that I can offer. But believe me when I say there is nothing else.'

'Except the estate; a valuable one, I believe.'

'Valuable? Shorecross?' Elizabeth snorted. 'It's been bankrupt for many years since my husband's father ran it into the ground. It would cost you to take it on, my lord.'

The earl frowned and looked at the list lying on his desk. 'I did hear the previous Lord Downes had financial difficulties.'

'Believe me, the estate it worthless. However, I can offer five hundred and fifty pounds in cash, immediately,' she said, 'and highly valuable land in Devon. The local monastery wants it, I believe, and is willing to pay high rents. Have you seen the price of wool? It's vanishing off the wharfs in Flanders. Your master is an astute business man, he wouldn't want to turn down such an investment. Shorecross won't earn any money until next year's harvest and sheep shearing, if then. In the meantime, it has over sixty freeborn workers who need feeding and their wages paid.'

She looked out of the window at the dark grey clouds threatening snow. 'I think it will be a long winter this year, and the harvest looks unprofitable.'

'Your husband committed a serious crime.'

'It was a war he shouldn't have been involved in. Edmund, the wool merchant, tricked you both for his own means. My husband returned because we were in danger.' She heard the passion in her own voice and looked down at her hands.

The steward narrowed his eyes and Elizabeth kept her head down as if she were unaware of his scrutiny. Under her day gown, her heart pounded. She thought of Will, then pushed his image from her mind, else she would become desperate and plead with this man for clemency.

'I'll think about your offer,' the man said.

'Thank you, my lord.' She dipped a curtsey and strode to the door, but he spoke again.

'You don't fool me, my lady. You pretend you don't care, but I see tears in your eyes and your hands are shaking. You love your husband dearly.'

Elizabeth turned around quickly, staring at the man standing behind his desk — at his lined cheeks and grizzled beard, eyes intelligent and all-seeing. She could not have fooled this man, not when he negotiated with the king and the great lords in the land.

'Please, I beg you, do not hang my husband. He is a good and brave man who would serve your master faithfully in the years to come. He has a strong sense of honour and duty, which is why he responded to your request, even though the border is far from our land. We are in this position due to another man's vengeance; it is not of our own making.'

'I don't execute men myself. That's the judgement of the courts and the king.'

'But the earl can drop the charges?'

'I'll write to my master; it's his decision.'

Elizabeth nodded. If she pressed further it might make him angry. All they could do now was hope.

★　★　★

'How long would it take to hear back from the earl?' Hugh said.

'I don't know.' Elizabeth looked up from the ledger she had placed on the desk. The offer had to be enough since she could find no more money. 'I want him home.' Putting her hands over her face, she sobbed, 'I should have given them Shorecross. What use is an estate to a dead man?'

'William would never have allowed you to give up the estate.' Hugh put his warm palm against her shoulder. 'You did everything you could.'

'If I hadn't agreed to marry Edmund, then none of this would have happened. Will could lose his life because he tried to protect me.'

'It was his whole family in danger, not just you. And Edmund was already involved with the family; look at what he did to Joan.'

Elizabeth nodded. She had forgotten that Edmund was Francis's father. Hugh had taken so well to the child, it was hard to remember that they were not actually related.

'I don't want to lose Will.' Her voice was little more than a whisper.

'None of us wants that.' He squeezed her shoulder. 'I'm sure we will hear soon.'

The door opened and she looked up at the earl's steward.

'News?' she said.

He shook his head. 'I'm leaving, mistress. There is no need for me to wait here. I'll send word of the earl's decision.'

'Please stay, I can't wait for another messenger.'

'I cannot. I'm needed at court.' He looked at her. 'I promise I will write immediately.'

'How long will it take?' Hugh said.

'I doubt it will be long, my master makes rapid choices. And with Lord Downes in the tower, time is of the essence since gaol fever is rife this time of year.'

Elizabeth moaned low in her throat.

'Have care for your words, sir. She had suffered enough,' Hugh said.

The man bowed. 'My apologies, my lady. I wish you all the best in saving your husband. I can understand why he took the action he did to protect you. If he doesn't return, please join us at court next year. You won't remain single for long.'

Hugh caught the ledger as Elizabeth grabbed and raised it.

'Calm, my lady,' he said. 'And sir, I suggest you find your horse.'

When the door closed, she rested against him. 'I can't bear it. What if they hang him?'

'I'm sure they won't.' But his eyes were dark and stricken.

★ ★ ★

Elizabeth stood by the window as the last of the sold sheep were led off to their new homes, bleating and racing after their shepherds. Yesterday, the cattle had gone, along with the winter hay supplies in the barn. With little livestock to feed, they had sold that as well. If Will returned, he would find a devastated farm.

She looked at the entrance to Shorecross. It had been two weeks since the message had gone to the earl, and they had heard nothing. Walter was on his way to London to seek news. Should she have gone as well? So desperate was her desire to see her husband, she would have risked the journey. But Margaret had refused to let her go. And she knew why. Her mother-in-law was fearful that she would have to watch the execution of Will.

Pressing her forehead against the glass, she stared out of the window. Was that a faint shout? But the lane beyond the curtain wall remained empty. Or did it? Something had moved; the trees stirred a little as if someone rode by. Or was it the wind and her imagination? No! There was movement: a dark object, likely the head of a horse, flashing in the air as if it tossed its neck. Could it be the messenger?

Grasping her skirts, Elizabeth raced down the stairs and out the front door.

'What is it?' Margaret shouted after her. 'Is there news?'

'I don't know!'

Panting, she stopped in the court-yard, staring at the gate. The portcullis remained firmly down, and the guards relaxed at their post. She must have imagined it, or else it was just a passing stranger using the lane to reach the village.

'Elizabeth? Did you see something?' Footsteps echoed behind her and she turned.

Margaret and Joan were hurrying across the courtyard, in the same manner as they had done when she arrived herself so many months ago.

Briefly, she closed her eyes, remembering the feel of Will's warm hands on her waist as he lifted her from the horse, the look in his eyes as he gazed at her before settling her down on her feet. She would give anything to be back in that time again.

'I hear a horse!' Joan said.

Elizabeth turned back to face the gate. Her sister-in-law was right; the thud of hooves came down the lane. How many horses? Would the messenger travel with others if he had bad news to impart? Lifting her skirts, she ran to the gate as the men began to pull up the heavy bars of the portcullis.

'Careful, mistress,' one of them said, as he hauled on the winding mechanism. 'You don't want to bang your head.'

'I don't care about that.' She peered into the lane, then, as soon as the gate had been lifted, slipped under it.

The lane was shaded with overgrown trees, allowing little light through. The clop of the hooves echoed down, closer and closer. The horse seemed to be speeding up, and she moved to the side as the unknown visitor reached the last corner. She stepped out, then leapt back as the horse reared in front of her, hooves high above her head.

Elizabeth flung herself onto the floor, rolling to the side. Tears in her eyes, she lay in the rotting, wet leaves. What a stupid thing to do! She would have angered the traveller. He might now change his mind about releasing her husband. The horse crashed back to the ground, then reared again, neighing. Oh, no! What if the rider was thrown off? She might have killed the man sent to tell her that Lord Downes had been freed. She might have harmed an innocent traveller by her foolish behaviour.

The animal's hooves thudded back onto the ground.

'I'm so sorry,' she said, her face against the leaves. 'Are you hurt?'

She attempted to turn over, but the unknown traveller dropped from his horse and laid a hand on her back.

'I seem to make a habit of rescuing you from horses,' he said.

'Will!' Elizabeth sat up. 'It's you! You're here!'

He smiled as he knelt in the mud beside her, his brown eyes tired, but filled with the love she remembered. His face was pale, a new scar across one cheek, and she raised a hand to gently touch it.

'You're alive,' she said, in wonder.

'I was released two days ago. I rode straight here.'

'I didn't think I would see you again.'

'I'm not that easy to get rid of.' Putting his hands under her knees, he lifted her up and she wrapped her arms around him, her head against his shoulder. 'It was the thought of you that kept me going. I had to live, because I couldn't bear to leave you. I love you, Elizabeth. You have brought such joy to my life, when I couldn't imagine ever being happy again.'

'I couldn't have lived without you,'

she said. 'It destroyed me to think of you suffering. You belong here at Shorecross.'

Will's lips pressed against hers and he kissed her deeply, clutching her tight against him. 'I'll never leave you again.' He drew his head back and smiled. 'I'll not let go of you.'

'That might make leading your horse in a little tricky,' she grinned.

Then footsteps sounded down the lane.

'I think we have reinforcements,' he said, as Margaret and Joan ran into view, their arms outstretched.

Epilogue

Elizabeth sat down on the warm step and waved away a fly. Sweat trickled down her breasts and she loosed the top tie of her gown, confident that no-one heeded her. In the field in front — the grass chewed low by sheep — she watched two little girls run, clutching their gowns up, dark curls loose in the sun.

'Mother!' the youngster shouted.

'I finished my work early,' Elizabeth said, and smiled as her two daughters grasped hands and raced off.

At first, she'd hoped to have many children, but the births had been difficult and after Mary five years ago, there had been no more. It did not worry her; two healthy, happy children was more then she had expected.

Looking up, she smiled. Will was striding across the grass towards her, linking arms along the way with his daughters. Behind him, mounted on his pony, Francis trotted. Elizabeth had been delighted when Hugh and Joan agreed to take one of the tenant farms of Shorecross. As Hugh pointed out, Francis needed to know the land if he was to inherit.

Elizabeth rose to her feet and took Mary's hand, and the four of them strode towards the manor house, from where the delicious smell of roasting lamb filled the air. Her days were filled with the joys of loving, and being loved, and she could imagine no richer life than to be here at Shorecross with her family.

Other titles in the
Linford Romance Library:

LUCY OF LARKHILL

Christina Green

Lucy is left to run her Dartmoor farm virtually on her own after a hired hand is injured. She does her best to carry on; though when she decides to sell her baked goods direct to the public, she is forced to admit that she is overwhelmed. She needs to hire a man to help on the farm, and her childhood friend Stephen might just be the answer. But as Lucy's feelings for him grow, she is more determined than ever to remain an independent spinster . . .

FINDING HER PERFECT FAMILY

Carol MacLean

Fleeing as far as she can from an unhappy home life, Amelia Knight arrives at the tropical island of Trinita to work as a nanny at the Grenville estate. As she battles insects and tropical heat, she must also fight her increasing attraction to baby Lucio's widowed father, Leo Grenville — a man whose heart has been broken, and thus is determined never to love again. Amelia must conquer stormy weather and reveal a desperate secret before she can find her perfect family to love forever.

THE SAPPHIRE

Fay Cunningham

Cass, a talented jeweller, wants a quiet life after having helped to solve a murder case. But life is anything but dull while she lives with her mother, an eccentric witch with a penchant for attracting trouble. Now Cass's father, who left the family when she was five, is back on the scene — as well handsome detective Noel Raven, with whom Cass has an electrifying relationship. As dangers both worldly and paranormal threaten Cass and those she loves, will they be strong enough to stand together and prevail?

TROUBLE IN PARADISE

Susan Udy

When Kat's mother, Ruth, tells her that her home and shop are under threat of demolition from wealthy developer Sylvester Jordan, Kat resolves to support her struggle to stay put. So when a mysterious vandal begins to target the shop, Sylvester — or someone in his employ — is their chief suspect. However, Sylvester is also offering Kat opportunities that will support her struggling catering business — and, worst of all, she finds that the attraction she felt to him in her school days is still very much alive . . .